BRIGHT CITY, SHATTERED

BRIGHT CITY, SHATTERED

Millie Abecassis

POLYMATH
— PRESS —

Aurora, CO

Bright City, Shattered by Millie Abecassis

This book is a work of fiction. All incidents, events, characters, names, business, places, and other entities depicted are either fictitious or are used fictitiously.

Copyright © 2025 by the author
Cover art: CreativeParamita
Author photograph: Clayton J. Mitchell
Design and layout: Robert Lewis

All rights reserved. No portion of this book may be reproduced in any form without written permission from the publisher or copyright holder.

Published by Polymath Press, a trade name of Polymath Enterprises, LLC. Please direct all inquiries to Polymath Press, P. O. Box 461870, Aurora, CO 80046-1870, online at www.polymathpress.com, or via email to editor@polymathpress.com.

First edition

ISBN (paperback): 978-1-961827-10-3
ISBN (eBook): 978-1-961827-11-0
Library of Congress Control Number: 2025938691

To Félix, the first to fall in
love with Bright City.

Also by Millie Abecassis

Daughters of the Blue Moon
(Anuci Press, February 2025)

Praise for *Daughters of the Blue Moon* by Millie Abecassis

"An alluring tale about the freedom to chase your fate and own your truth. If this story doesn't inspire you to live life on your own terms, I don't know what will." — **Chris Campeau**, author of *Resisters*

"A dark and twisted fairy tale with betrayal and family secrets as sharp as the knives the strong and defiant heroine uses on the wolves haunting the heart of the woods." — **Yolanda Sfetsos**, author of *Only Darkness*

On the day Reine got her dream job, Papa lost his leg.

Reine sat in the office of Max Caldwell, the CEO of Clean Crystal Corporation—C3 for short—when the sirens went off. She had heard them several times in her life, and they always filled her with a deep, instinctive fear that men like Max Caldwell would never understand.

"The wall will protect us," Caldwell said.

Reine stared through the window wall, her eyes fixed on the horizon.

"I have personally contributed to its maintenance for over twenty years," he continued. "It will protect the city."

"I know," Reine said. Everyone knew the wall protected the city and she was no exception. "I'm worried about the people beyond."

"Ah. Family?"

She nodded. "Pearl divers."

"A risky but rewarding occupation," Caldwell said as he touched the thin necklace around his neck made of black and white pearls.

It must have cost him a fortune, Reine thought, and she didn't know how to feel about it. Her family depended on the elite's demand for pearls to make a living, but that elite was also happy to ignore pearl divers' struggles with middlemen and jewelers always pressuring them for lower prices.

Caldwell cleared his throat. "Do you need to take a break? Make some calls, maybe?"

Reine glanced at the shiny white phone on the desk, the latest model combining an answering machine, a cordless handset, a fax machine, and a color digital screen. Another fortune. "No, it's fine. There's nothing I can do from here." If she could hear the sirens, then Mama could hear them too. She looked at Max Caldwell and clasped her hands. "I can only hope my father isn't at sea right now."

"I hope so, too. And he won't need to be at sea in the future, anyway."

"What do you mean, Mr. Caldwell?"

He smiled from ear to ear. "You got the job. And call me Max, please. Welcome to C3, Reine."

Bright City, Shattered

Reine hailed a taxi.

"Sea-gate number four, please," she said, entering the car.

"Are you deaf or what?" the driver asked, removing a cassette from his car's built-in player. "There's a wave coming. A bad one."

"Yeah, I know."

"So, you know the gate must be closed by now, right?"

Reine nodded.

"And you still want to go there?"

She nodded again.

"I'm not driving near the wall with a wave coming."

"You don't trust the wall?"

"I trust my guts, and they tell me not to go near the wall when the sirens are wailing like the heavens are falling."

"I'll give you a generous tip."

"Oh yeah? A rich lady, eh?"

"Just got hired at C3."

The driver looked at Reine in his rear-view mirror. "You're one of those enmagineers?"

Reine shook her head and lifted her sunglasses, revealing plain brown eyes. "I'm their new head of security."

The driver sneered. "You're in charge of security at C3 and you want me to drive toward the wall when there's a wave coming? You're a joke, ma'am, you know."

Reine sighed. The car hadn't moved since their little chat had started. "Are you going to take me there or not?"

"Nah. Get out of my car."

Reine didn't say a word and complied with the request.

"You shouldn't go there, ma'am," the driver said through the window.

"I know."

The driver shook his head, shrugged, and drove away.

Reine watched the car pull away, then she walked toward the sea.

The wave hit the shore with brute force. It was one of the worst waves that had reached the city in the last twenty years, the kind that annihilated everything but the wall.

The wall stood strong. The city was safe.

It'd always been safe from the sea and the forest and the ground—even from the sky. From everything. All people had to do was live inside it. The city couldn't promise more. It couldn't promise its people a proper home, a decent income, or even food. All it could promise was safety…and power. Cheap, reliable power for everyone, provided by C3 and by the miracles of enmagineering.

Everybody had a fridge powered by C3, even if they had nothing to put in it.

Reine found Mama and Nola at the shelter near the fourth sea-gate. Nola sobbed in Mama's arms, her small portable computer under one elbow. *She must have grabbed it before fleeing the house,* Reine thought. It was Nola's most valuable possession. An old model, but she needed it for her studies. It was all she had besides a small shoulder bag. She glanced at Reine and wiped her tears with the back of her hand.

"Where's Papa?" Reine asked.

Nola sniffed. "He's…he's at the hospital."

"A whistling whale got him," Mama whispered.

"Shit," Reine blurted, running her hand through her cropped hair. The family house was probably gone, swept away by the wave—or at least damaged beyond repair—but it didn't matter. A whale attacked Papa. Even if he recovered from his injuries, he would never dive again.

"They came with the wave…vicious beasts!" Nola hissed.

The whales had always been a threat to fishermen and pearl divers, but the waves, caused by distant earthquakes, made it worse. The whales liked to follow them and rip apart anyone in the water. They came furtively before stunning their oblivious victims with a high-pitched, deafening whistle. A pearl diver deep in the ocean, unaware of the sirens wailing at the surface, was easy prey for the beasts. Even though Papa always dived with a harpoon—and he'd repelled whales several times—it seemed he hadn't been able to defend himself this time.

"He's undergoing surgery. He lost a leg, and a lot of blood. The doctors said he'll live."

Reine blinked. This was supposed to be a good day. When Papa had kissed her goodbye in the morning, he had that large, beaming smile on his face and said, "I'll find a huge, gleaming pearl today, and it'll be yours if you get the job."

Now, his leg was in the belly of a whale, the rest of his body on an operating table, and the promised pearl safe inside its shell at the bottom of the sea.

Reine awoke with a start to the shrill sound of the alarm clock. Cursing, she slammed the snooze button to stop the irritating noise and swiftly switched the alarm off.

She hated alarm clocks, but no one else would wake her up, hammering on the bedroom door like Nola used to do when they all still lived together in the family beach house.

There was no house anymore.

Instead, there was this small, unfamiliar apartment

where she moved in a week ago. With her new job at C3, she could afford a bigger place where they could all live together again, but Mama insisted that she take her own place. In return, Reine found another place for Papa, Mama and Nola, so they wouldn't have to stay at the shelter and Papa could leave the hospital and recover at home.

So she found them a large apartment in a building in the Big District and picked a small studio for herself where she could almost touch each wall from the center of its only room. She could have afforded something bigger for herself, but there was Papa's rehab to pay for, and that wasn't cheap. Even if they'd made good money selling pearls, they were now using their savings to buy clothes, furniture, and everything else they'd lost to the wave. With Papa unable to work, Mama taking care of him, and Nola still going to computer science school, Reine's sign-on bonus and soon-to-be-paid salary were the only things preventing them from ending up in the slums.

Max Caldwell had been right. Papa wouldn't have to dive anymore. C3 made it possible, and the whale made it certain.

Reine made coffee using the brand-new electric kettle and plunger coffee pot she bought the day before. She grimaced as she took a sip. Why did she buy a coffee pot? She didn't even like coffee. She always preferred tea, but Mama would always make pot after pot of coffee every day and wouldn't fill Reine's cup with anything else for breakfast, barely allowing her to add sugar or milk.

But Mama wasn't there, so Reine poured some milk into her cup and almost enjoyed her coffee.

Today was her first day at C3.

She put on the security uniform C3 sent her two days ago. The company logo, a diamond-shaped crystal, was embroidered on the black shirt.

Reine looked through the window at the C3 Tower. Like almost everyone else in the city, she could see the tower from her apartment. It was the tallest one and its characteristic blue light, emitted by the crystal at the top, made it impossible to miss, even in broad daylight. How could anyone ignore the crystal, anyway? It was everywhere in the city: in lightbulbs, fridges, ovens, TVs, cars, in the city's subway and taxis—in everything that needed electricity. "A miracle technology," C3's founder Florence Caldwell called it when she unveiled it forty years ago, her face and quote still displayed in C3's lobby for everyone to admire.

And a miracle it still was. In a way, it was life itself.

Reine stood in the lobby for less than five minutes before the receptionist called her name. She was the same red-haired and snub-nosed woman that had welcomed her two weeks ago for her interview with Max Caldwell, with pale green eyes almost as bright as the sky-blue of an enmagineer's, and a name tag reading "Allie" pinned onto her chest.

"Welcome to C3," Allie said with a cheery, fruity voice. "Here is your badge. Emyr Evenson, our Personnel Director, will receive you in an instant."

Allie didn't lie because Evenson appeared in the lobby right after she finished her sentence. He was a big man with large hands that could have easily crushed Reine's if he wasn't also very gentle when they shook hands. His face was as gentle as his temperament, and he smiled the whole time they met.

They'd spent barely twenty minutes together, Reine signing documents as a photocopier spewed them out, when a woman knocked at the door and opened it before Evenson could answer.

"Am I early?" she asked with the silveriest voice Reine had ever heard.

"Never," Evenson said, and Reine could only agree with him.

The woman wore a lab coat tightly buttoned over a brown dress, and her large, rounded eyes were that shiny, unique sky-blue shade only enmagineers possessed—a consequence of their ability to see and control luma, the once-unexploitable natural resource flowing through the air, the forest, and the sea that C3 managed to encapsulate in its miraculous crystal. It wasn't only her eyes that gave her a soft yet imposing presence; the way she stood, too, told Reine that she was an important person at C3.

She was right, because the woman said, "I'm Isaline Caldwell, the lab director," and Reine knew exactly who she was. Not only the lab director, but also Max Caldwell's niece and one of the most brilliant enmagineers of her generation. "You can call me Isaline."

"I'm—"

"Reine, I know," Isaline said with a soft smile. "Max asked me to give you a tour of the labs."

Evenson snorted and said, "I'm sure you'll find it way more interesting than our paperwork."

Reine found the lab tour interesting indeed, and Isaline even more.

She had already met enmagineers, but none compared to her. Isaline wasn't only smart; she was also passionate about her job and kind enough to explain it patiently to someone like Reine who knew nothing about enmagineering. Even the dullest captors, screens, and machines became intriguing as Isaline explained the crucial research her team conducted.

"Thanks to luma enmagineering, the crystal provides us with a clean, safe, sustainable, and immensely efficient source of energy," she said. "But we can always do better. With the city population growing, we need to produce more energy, as clean as it's always been."

Reine nodded as she listened quietly to every word coming out of Isaline's mouth.

"What were you doing before joining C3?" Isaline asked. "You're quite young to lead the security of an entire company."

You're young to lead a lab, too, Reine wanted to answer, but Isaline was right. Isaline's reputation preceded her, but Reine's didn't. There weren't many enmagineers as bright as Isaline in the city, but there were plenty of good leaders in the Bright City Defense.

"I served in the BCD for ten years. Did the mandatory year when I turned eighteen and decided to serve a bit longer. I didn't know how long I'd stay, then I ended up training new recruits, and not long after, I was leading an entire unit. I was based near woods-gate number two."

"Oh, I see," Isaline said before falling silent. She must have known how hard it was to lead a team in the BCD. Enmagineers weren't required to serve in the BCD, their skills being in high demand and their safety not worth the risk, but Isaline must have known people—family members, friends—who had been among these difficult-to-lead recruits who didn't want to leave the city to patrol the forest bordering the city's south.

Reine wouldn't blame any of the new recruits she'd trained over her years in the BCD, because the animals in the forest weren't just wild. Like the whistling whales, they tracked, attacked, and killed people, and few citizens dared to leave the city without a BCD escort. The beasts' fangs were so long, their claws so sharp, and their skin so thick that BCD agents had to use power guns created by enmagineers to repel them.

"I quit last year," Reine continued. "I liked my job, but it was grueling, and I couldn't see my family as much as I'd wanted. I'd been thinking about it for about a year before making my decision."

"What convinced you to quit?"

"A pack of razor-toothed wolves ambushed my unit. I almost lost three men that day. We all made it back alive, but that was the last straw."

Isaline sighed. "I don't understand why those beasts are so aggressive. What have we done to them? They've got the entire forest to themselves and plenty of prey to hunt."

"I don't know," Reine said, shaking her head. "After that, I told my superior that I'd been proud to serve in the BCD and that it was time to pass on the torch to someone else. I was honorably discharged, then I moved back in with my parents and looked for a new job while helping with the family business."

"A wise decision. Your family could have lost you. They must be so relieved to know you're working at C3 now."

Reine considered telling Isaline about her family's dangerous occupation, and that she'd almost lost her father to a whale, but instead she just nodded and said, "The pay at the BCD was decent, but not as good as what I'll be making at C3."

"Max is very generous," was all Isaline answered.

Later in the morning, Isaline took Reine to the thirtieth and highest floor. Reine was going to see the crystal, and not from afar. She was going to see the real thing in all its glory in the Core Room.

Isaline gave her goggles. "It would blind you," she said as Reine was about to ask why she needed them. "You're not an enmagineer, and your eyes can't look at the crystal at such a close distance without going blind in a few minutes."

It made sense, like everything Isaline said. Reine put on the goggles while Isaline badged to open the door, then followed the lab director into the Core Room.

And there she saw it.

A huge diamond-shaped crystal, two floors high, floating in the center of a circular room larger than her now-gone two-story family beach house. The light was indeed blinding and Reine wondered if the goggles were enough to protect her eyesight, because she had to squint so hard her eyelids hurt after only a minute. As for Isaline, she stared at it with naked eyes. Reine wondered how this was possible, even with sky-blue enmagineer eyes.

The light wasn't the only eerie thing about the crystal. She didn't know how to describe it, but the crystal *hummed*. It was a low, persistent sound that she could not only hear but also feel in her bones, in her flesh, on her skin. Her entire body resonated with the crystal.

Reine heard Isaline whisper something incomprehensible as she was facing the crystal. "Say that again?" she asked. "The…humming makes it hard to hear you from behind."

Isaline turned to her with a surprised look. Then she blinked and said, raising her voice, "What you call the humming, we call the murmur. It's just the noise of luma being processed by the crystal. Completely normal and safe. The light is dangerous to non-enmagineers' eyes, but the murmur isn't loud enough to damage your eardrums."

"I see," Reine said. "It's…I've never heard anything like it."

Isaline nodded. "The crystal truly is one of a kind."

Reine walked toward the crystal, but Isaline put a hand on her shoulder, gently but also firmly. "Don't go any closer."

"I thought the crystal was safe."

Isaline hesitated for a second, and it surprised Reine to see such a knowledgeable woman waver. More surprising was the fear that flashed in her eyes. Was she scared of the crystal? But before Reine could ask what was happening, Isaline said, "Safe from a distance. Please, stay back."

Reine kept her question to herself and nodded. She would have to learn a lot about the lab safety, and she was happy at the thought of learning it from Isaline.

"It used to be so small," Isaline continued. "Smaller than a stone on an engagement ring when my grandmother founded C3. And now look at it! We fed it with the best luma, and it gives us a virtually endless supply of energy."

Reine was looking at it, and it was beautiful. As beautiful as the smile Isaline gave her when they walked outside of the Core Room.

"Sorry for interrupting."

Reine looked up at the security office doorway and met Isaline's gaze. She glanced at the wall clock that showed

5:50. "No, you're fine. I was about to leave soon, anyway."

Isaline smiled. "I just ran into Max before he left the office. He asked me to ask you if you were available for a dinner with the team the day after tomorrow?"

"I…yes," Reine stuttered. "I'd love to have dinner with you. And the team."

"Great. The reservation is at Five Hills, at six. It's right down the street."

"I'll be there."

Isaline moved to leave, but she stopped. "Actually, do you have time right now?"

"For dinner?" Reine said very fast.

"Oh, no," Isaline said, and Reine felt stupid for asking. "That'd be lovely, but I've got a lot of work today, and I have no idea when I'm going to leave." She tilted her head. "I'd like to show you a…special place in the office. Do you like coffee?"

Reine considered lying and pretending she was the biggest coffee enthusiast in the city, but instead she said, nodding, "I enjoy coffee in the morning."

"What do you say of good coffee with a great view?"

"That sounds nice."

Isaline winked before saying, "Follow me."

Reine didn't need to be asked twice and followed Isaline to the elevator, where she frowned in surprise as Isaline pressed the "29" button. Max Caldwell's office was on the twenty-ninth floor.

The elevator swiftly slid to the top of the building, taking a quiet but excited Reine to Isaline's *special place*. Whatever it was, Reine couldn't help but feel special, too. Isaline was a busy woman, yet she had shown her the labs and the Core Room in the morning, and now she was taking more time to show her C3's secret corners.

"This way," Isaline said as they left the elevator and walked past Max Caldwell's office.

Isaline's special place was a break room hidden in a corner of the twenty-ninth floor. A leather couch and designer chairs faced a flat-screen TV that displayed images of a burning fireplace. Between the TV and the seats, a solid wood round table stood on a brown carpet emboldened with intricate golden patterns. The TV alone must have cost three months of Reine's salary, and the furniture seemed to come from a luxury store whose products she could never afford.

"The coffee machine is actually more expensive than everything else combined," Isaline said, as if she had read Reine's mind like an open book. She gestured toward a tall black machine that looked like it came from the future. Reine had never seen such a complex thing, and all it made was…coffee?

Isaline met Reine's perplexed gaze and said, "It makes *very good* coffee," then she grabbed two porcelain cups from the cupboard. "How do you want it?"

"Long," Reine stuttered. "With milk. Please."

"As you wish," Isaline responded, pressing the buttons to program the machine.

Reine observed the machine brewing that bitter drink she didn't even like, and asked, "Are all employees allowed to come here?"

"Yes, if you don't mind running into Max when he's on edge," Isaline said, putting Reine's coffee aside and programming the machine to brew a second one. "He likes to come here to relax after he's had a tough conversation with our shareholders or whoever has made him unhappy." She tilted her head, still looking at the coffee machine. "In truth, nobody dares come up here."

"Except you."

Isaline laughed softly. "Except me. The coffee and the view are worth it."

Reine approached the window wall. Far below, she could see the city and dozens of pedestrians that looked like ants. They were crawling through the streets, going back home after a long workday, running errands, or doing only heavens knew what. Above them were the imposing silhouettes of Bright City's buildings and the countless birds nesting in their alcoves. Reine could even see the city wall in the distance and the ocean beyond it. She was seeing it for the first time since the wave hit Bright City's shore. Unidentifiable debris still covered parts of the coast—the family beach house somewhere among them, Reine thought, trying not to wince.

She looked back at the center of the city and caught a glimpse of the city hall, a pyramidal building whose construction had just begun when Reine joined the BCD, and ended less than two years later, right on time for the new mayor-president to settle in. Next to it were headquarters of the rapidly growing telecommunication companies. If their billboard ads were to be believed, their newer, better personal digital assistants would soon make landlines a thing of the past.

At last, Reine looked toward the forest, where she had spent most of the last decade. Few buildings sat beyond the wall—just some BCD outposts and a warehouse belonging to Timberlight, Bright City's only forestry company. It was heavily guarded by BCD personnel, and Reine herself had protected lumberjacks from wildlife countless times. Fortunately for the men and women of Timberlight, they spent little time chopping trees, as the company's recycling division was far more developed than the one producing paper from freshly cut wood. The forest was simply too dangerous. Even BCD personnel slept in barracks on the safe side of the city wall, next to the farms and greenhouses that produced half of the food the citizens consumed—the other half coming from fishing and kelp farming.

Bright City's divisions had never been so visible to Reine as from the top of the C3 Tower, which stood at the center of the city. It looked like an onion: a dry outer layer that protected the tender inside ones, and at its center, the roots, feeding every layer with much-needed energy.

"Such a precious city."

The words snapped Reine out of her reflection. She hadn't noticed Isaline joining her in her contemplation. She nodded and whispered, "Yes. Yes, it is."

"Coffee is ready," Isaline said, pointing at the table where two steaming cups waited for them.

They sat on the designer chairs, facing each other.

Reine lifted her cup and sipped some coffee. It felt sweet and buttery, as she'd never experienced before. The taste was so unusual that she raised her eyebrows and Isaline said, "I told you it was good coffee."

"It's…delicious, yes," she admitted.

"The real milk helps, too," Isaline added. "It's not like the powdered one in the other machines." She brought her own cup to her lips and drank it down.

Reine cleared her throat. "Thanks again for the tour this morning."

"Oh, of course," Isaline said, putting down her empty cup. "It was my pleasure. I could speak about enmagineering for hours…though, I'm sure that'd become really boring really fast."

Reine could have listened to Isaline talk about anything for hours, no matter how boring the topic, simply to hear her voice and admire her face lightning up with passion, so she said, "No, it was interesting."

Isaline chuckled. "You are way too polite, Reine."

"No, no, I mean it. The crystal, in particular, was fascinating."

Isaline nodded. "To think we barely understand it…. Oh, don't get me wrong," she said, as Reine frowned at her in surprise. "We know what we're doing, but we don't understand *why* it works. My grandmother's creation is a miracle. Using enmagineering to channel luma into that fantastic crystal…only a brilliant mind like hers could have come up with that idea and made it a reality." She sighed and gave Reine a faint melancholic smile. Then she glanced at her watch and said, standing up, "I'm sorry, but I have to run. You can stay here if you want to enjoy the view a little longer."

"Thanks for showing me this place," Reine said, nodding. "It truly is special." *Like you,* she wanted to add but kept to herself.

"I'm glad you like it. All right, I *really* have to go. I'll see you around tomorrow, and if not, at dinner the following day."

"I look forward to it."

"Likewise. Have a good evening, Reine."

And with that, Isaline walked away and disappeared into the corridor, leaving Reine alone with her sweet coffee and sweeter feelings.

The next morning, Reine woke up right before the time she had scheduled the alarm clock to ring. She deactivated it, put on her C3 uniform, and went to the kitchen.

It had only one cooking appliance, a small hotplate squeezed in between the sink and the fridge, but it was all Reine needed to make a rolled omelet—her favorite dish. Eggs were expensive, but nothing would stop Reine from starting her second day at C3 with a delicious breakfast. She even added green onions and rainbow tuna.

A smile spread on her face as she took a first bite, but not only because the omelet tasted good. She was thinking about Isaline, too. She couldn't wait to meet her again in the office, and tomorrow for dinner.

Her omelet gobbled up, Reine started to wash the dishes when her phone rang. She dried her hands rapidly and picked up the call. Immediately, she recognized her boss's voice.

"Reine, we have a problem," Caldwell said very fast, and her stomach dropped when he added, "It's Isaline.

She's dead."

The police were already there when Reine arrived at the C3 Tower. Journalists, too, already harassing the employees and speculating on what happened inside the walls of Bright City's most important company. Reine ignored them as they shouted at her. She knew they would soon find out her name and the nature of her employment at C3, and it would be in all newspapers, but the only thing that mattered at that moment was Isaline.

Was she really dead? Reine had been on the job for only one day, and the worst had already happened. And it had happened to *her*. To Isaline.

Max Caldwell was in the lobby, talking to a police officer close to the reception desk where Allie frantically picked up calls and put people on hold, with a voice not cheery or fruity at all.

As Reine approached Caldwell, he told Allie, "Just turn on the damn after hours voicemail." He gave her an annoyed glance that she returned, then he looked up at Reine. "There you are. Reine, this is Detective Inspector Novau. He'll be leading the investigation into Isaline's murder."

"Murder?" Reine asked, frowning. Did a violent intruder attack Isaline? Or was it an employee? Why hadn't her team informed her that a dangerous person was on the company premises? Had they failed to neutralize the individual before the worst happened? Had the person been arrested? What in heavens happened?

"That's what your boss leans toward," Novau replied with a hoarse voice. The man had either an awful cold or a serious smoking problem, and looking at the deep lines around his lips and the loose skin under his eyes, Reine bet on smoking. "But we're not excluding other causes yet. It could be an accident, or else."

So there hadn't been an intruder, Reine realized, half relieved and half confused. They didn't know what had happened.

Caldwell sighed and briefly shook his head, then he said, "Reine, I'll need you to assist Novau with the investigation. Make sure he gets access to our CCTV recordings, can interview employees…whatever he needs to find the culprit. I want my niece's murderer found and put behind bars." His voice was sharp, and he sounded more irritated than truly angry or sad, as Reine would expect someone to be after losing a close family member. Maybe he had a hard time realizing this was happening, and that Isaline was dead.

He wouldn't be the only one, because Reine couldn't believe it either.

Reine soon found out that Isaline's death was all too awfully real.

Novau escorted her to the perhaps-crime, perhaps-accident scene in the Core Room. He asked her questions about her encounter with Isaline and her whereabouts the previous night, taking notes in a brown leather book as the elevator took them to the thirtieth floor, while assuring her she wasn't a suspect.

When the elevator door opened, Novau handed her goggles. She absentmindedly put them on, her thoughts focused on the complete nonsense she was going through. Isaline, dead in the Core Room, on her second day at C3. It couldn't be real. No, Novau was surely walking her to a very alive Isaline, and they would soon tell her it was a test to assess her reaction and confirm her hiring.

But it wasn't. Isaline's dead body was right behind the Core Room's door and visible to anybody coming that way. A door stopper allowed evidence technicians to walk in and out, also causing the crystal's blinding light to flood the corridor.

Everybody except one blue-eyed technician wore goggles. Reine wondered why an enmagineer worked for the police. They all worked for C3 or its subsidiaries, or for some start-up pretending it would revolutionize the city and outshine C3. But this one seemed to have chosen a different path. A path that didn't include the use of his enmagineering skills. Why not, after all? Nola had the most beautiful voice Reine had ever heard, yet she had no interest in entering the annual Bright City Talent Contest—sponsored by C3, like half of the city's events—to become the next superstar singer. Reine herself was such a good diver, she could have worked with Papa to collect pearls if she had wanted to. But she didn't want to, and that's probably what that police technician told himself, too, when offered the opportunity to work for C3.

Novau said, "She was found like this"—he looked at his watch—"about an hour ago."

The goggleless technician walked to Novau and said, glancing at Reine, "We're done taking pictures and collecting evidence." He gestured around him. "There wasn't much to find. The room and corridor are completely normal, except for Ms. Caldwell's body. There's no blood and no visible injury or trauma on her body at first review. We'll still have to see what the autopsy and toxicology say, of course."

Novau nodded before exhaling noisily. "Run every test. I don't want the culprit to get away with murdering Max Caldwell's niece."

Reine was tempted to ask why he was, like Max

Caldwell, already talking about murder when there was no conclusive evidence at that point—barely any evidence at all, it seemed—but she looked at Isaline's body and felt her blood turn to ice when she met her eyes. Even in death, they were still vividly sky-blue. They were so blue, it seemed they radiated light. Like the crystal itself.

Novau stood behind Reine silently as they reviewed the CCTV recordings of the past hours together. There was no recording from inside the Core Room, since CCTV cameras couldn't handle the crystal's effects—and, Reine would quickly learn, because enmagineers hated being monitored.

They only had recordings from the cameras in the corridor leading to the Core Room, and all they could see after reviewing them was Isaline walking into the Core Room at ten thirty in the evening, and Udo Elante, the lab team manager and Isaline's right hand, walking in at six in the morning to find her dead.

"Are we sure she was alone in there?" Novau asked.

Reine went back further in time, until she saw herself walking inside with Isaline around eleven in the morning and leaving the Core Room a few minutes later. Nobody else had come in or out between then and Isaline's evening visit.

"It seems I'm the last person who went into the Core Room with Isaline."

Novau glanced at Reine and frowned a little. "What did you two do inside?"

"She just showed me the crystal," Reine answered very fast, feeling herself blush unexpectedly. Perhaps she worried about being considered a suspect, she thought. That, or something else she didn't understand. "Nothing more."

"Was there someone else working in the Core Room, maybe?"

Reine shook her head. "No. We were alone."

"Are you certain?"

"I didn't see anyone else. I can go back further in time if you want, but I doubt we'll see anybody getting in and not getting out. That thing—the crystal—it's intense. Even with goggles, you couldn't stay long inside without going blind or insane."

Novau shrugged. "It could be another enmagineer."

"Another enmagineer hiding all day in the Core Room until they can murder Isaline?"

"We can't eliminate any lead."

"Nobody has left the Core Room since Isaline walked in. The only person to get in was Elante, and we can see on the recording that he found her dead." Reine sped up the video to the moment Elante found Isaline, tapping the screen with her finger to show Novau how Isaline's body was already lying on the floor when Elante opened the door. Even with the crystal's light altering the quality of the recording, Isaline's body was visible enough to exonerate Elante.

"Hmm," Novau grumbled. "What did he do *after* that?"

"After?"

"Yes. Keep moving forward."

The video showed Elante calling Isaline, then approaching her after she failed to respond, and putting his face above hers, visibly checking if she was breathing. After a few seconds, the video showed him rise, staggering a little, then rush to the elevator. Reine checked the videos from the other floors and saw Elante leaving the elevator on the twenty-ninth floor and running into Max Caldwell's office. Caldwell and Elante emerged shortly thereafter, and both went to the elevator. Reine switched back to the thirtieth floor and saw Caldwell rushing to the Core Room and kneeling next to Isaline's body, checking her neck for a pulse, but Elante wasn't with him anymore. Reine looked at the other floors and found Elante had gone to the fifteenth floor, to the office of Araya Lancy, the director of health and safety. The video showed him knocking on the door, entering the unlocked office, leaving after a brief moment, and going back to the elevator alone. Lancy and her team weren't in the office yet.

"Why did he run to that office?" Novau asked.

"Ms. Lancy is our director of health and safety, and she's also a nurse. Perhaps Elante thought Isaline wasn't dead and could receive medical help?"

"Why not call an ambulance right away?"

"He must have panicked," Reine guessed. "People do that when they've never been in that situation." She had seen so many recruits in the BCD act completely erratically when faced with an injured or dead teammate despite their training that Elante's reaction didn't surprise her.

"Maybe," Novau said. "I'll make sure someone in my team asks him." Reine frowned and he added, "We are currently interviewing him."

"Is he a suspect?"

"He's an important witness but could become a suspect depending on how the interview goes." He cleared his throat. "How many enmagineers work at C3?"

"You would have to ask Mr. Evenson, our personnel director."

Novau nodded and wrote something down in his notebook. "Are there other ways to leave the Core Room other than the door? An air vent or a back door? What about the windows?"

Reine shook her head. The previous day, before having coffee with Isaline, she had spent several hours reviewing plans of the building, studying the labs and the Core Room in particular. There was only one way in and out. Air vents in the Core Room were too tiny even for a small child and covered by grates made of steel so thick a small robot couldn't have pierced them. As for the laminated glass windows, they were all fixed windows whose sole purpose was to spread the crystal's light in the city for aesthetic purposes. Breaking one was near impossible, not to mention the craziness of climbing the tower from a lower floor. At this height, the winds blowing constantly over the city would have swept anyone to their death. The only things leaving the room were the dozens of cables capturing the crystal's energy at its very top, and they all went through extremely thin tubes.

"No," Reine said, explaining what she knew about the Core Room to Novau. "If someone murdered Isaline, they did something to her *before* she walked inside the Core Room." She paused, thinking about her next words. Gulping, she continued, "Or it was an accident. She was close to the crystal, and—"

"The crystal is safe," Novau said, waving his hand dismissively. "It's never harmed anyone before. Isn't that what your company is so proud of?"

Reine remained silent, remembering what Isaline had told her. Yes, the crystal was safe, but *from a distance.*

The guard rail prevented anybody from going too close, but Isaline stopped Reine from getting closer before she touched it. And that hesitation…Isaline was *wary* of the crystal. But what Novau had said was true, too. After her lab tour, Reine had met with Lancy, who shared the history of incidents since the company's creation. Since the crystal's inception, it hadn't harmed anyone, and she had joked that she would be jobless if her sole duty was to protect employees from it. The only incidents that ever happened all took place in the labs, or on the office floors, outside of the Core Room.

But what if the crystal wasn't safe *anymore?*

When was the last safety test done? Reine wondered. Elante would know, but the police were questioning him. Lancy would know, then.

She rose from her chair, about to leave, but Novau cleared his throat noisily. "Do you have everything you need from me, detective?" she asked.

Novau scratched his head. "I'll just need copies of the past forty-eight hours of recordings so my team can examine them."

Reine nodded and said, "Consider it done."

"The last safety test is from this morning, around

four," Lancy said. She pushed her glasses up. "Isaline ran three tests, actually. One at midnight…another one at one-thirty, and the last one at four, before she…before…."

Silence filled Lancy's office.

Lancy gulped noisily. She couldn't finish her sentence, and neither could Reine. Isaline's death still seemed unreal, even after Reine saw Isaline's body and met her disturbingly shiny dead blue eyes. She had seen death many times, but this felt different. Isaline wasn't supposed to be in danger. She wasn't diving in a whistling whale-infested ocean. She wasn't patrolling the forest. She wasn't supposed to die.

"What did the tests say?" Reine asked quietly.

Lancy typed on her keyboard while looking intensely at her screen. "They all gave normal results. No perturbations in the pulsations, resonance, luma flow, or stability of the crystal. Everything was good, as usual. Even better than usual." She opened her eyes wide. "It was…perfect."

Reine sighed. "How does—how *did* Isaline run the tests? Is it dangerous? Did she need to get close to the crystal?"

Lancy shook her head. "No, it's not dangerous. She ran everything from the console in the small control station inside the Core Room. It takes a lot of energy to run the test, so that's why you see the crystal twinkle occasionally from outside, but it's completely safe from the console. Even if you'd be standing next to the crystal when running the test, as long as you're behind the guardrail, it would be safe in theory."

"In theory?"

"You must be at the console to start the test."

"Could someone else run the test from the console while Isaline was standing too close to the crystal?"

"Udo could—he runs the tests when Isaline isn't available—but he wouldn't. That would be against safety protocols."

And Elante wasn't in the Core Room with Isaline, so this wouldn't lead anywhere.

"What do the results look like, typically?" Reine asked.

Lancy frowned. "I'm not sure you would understand if I showed them to you. It's basically a lot of curves and percentages."

"Who receives the reports?"

"Udo, Isaline, and myself. And Max—he gets copies of all reports, even if he never looks at them."

"So," Reine said, "Isaline spent several hours all by herself in the Core Room, running three safety tests in the middle of the night before walking away, only to drop dead as she was reaching the door."

Lancy gave her a confused look and a feeble smile that meant she didn't have a better explanation to offer. Then she said, "The only thing I can say, if it helps, is that Isaline had *never* run two or more safety tests in a row before."

Novau and his team didn't waste their time. Barely forty-eight hours after Elante found Isaline dead in the Core Room, Novau shared the results of the autopsy with Max Caldwell, Lancy and Reine.

"She died of sudden cardiac arrest," he said. "Her medical history showed that she had Pabst's disease, like many highly gifted enmagineers."

"Handling high quantities of luma can cause some unfortunate side effects," Lancy explained as she noticed Reine's frowned eyebrows.

"I thought luma was safe," Reine said.

"It is, but even the safest substance can become poisonous at high doses. Enmagineers handle a thousand times more luma than we regular people have in our bodies. Fortunately, most are unharmed by it thanks to their natural abilities, but some less fortunate enmagineers like Isaline develop Pabst's disease."

"She was receiving the best treatment on the market for it," Caldwell said. "It was completely under control. Her heart was working completely fine."

"The toxicology showed that, yes," Novau said. "It also showed borderline results for copsiamine."

"Copsiamine?" Reine asked. Considering the looks the others were giving her, she felt like she was supposed to know what it was, but she didn't. She was no physician, or chemist, or luma expert.

"Copsiamine is used to treat several conditions. In Isaline's case, it's the active ingredient of the main drug used to manage Pabst's disease," Lancy explained. "It helps regulate the natural electric currents of the body so the nervous system, the brain, the heart—everything, basically—can work normally. But too much of it is bad, too. For affected enmagineers, it's all about finding the right balance between luma and copsiamine."

Reine frowned. "Could she have mistakenly taken more than the normal dose?"

"Isaline wasn't like that," Caldwell said. "She monitored her treatment to perfection. She wouldn't have ever made that mistake."

"Even so," Lancy said, "you would have to take more than a double or triple dose to get in trouble. An overdose would only be int—"

"She wouldn't overdose intentionally," Caldwell snapped. "Isaline had everything she wished in life and no reason to commit suicide."

"We searched her apartment and didn't find a suicide note or anything of that sort," Novau said.

"Of course. She was the most balanced person I ever

knew," Caldwell continued. "No, she's been poisoned by someone who knew her condition. That's fucking it and we all know it."

Reine didn't *know it*, neither did she know anything about Pabst's disease, and she wasn't a detective either, but she offered, "I don't think we can rule out the safety accident completely. I know the crystal is supposed to be safe, but she—"

"What are you suggesting, Reine?" Caldwell said, almost shouting. "That the crystal caused her to have a cardiac arrest?"

"There was no sign of electrocution," Novau said. "The medical examiner didn't find burns or organ damage caused by electricity."

"There is no electricity in the Core Room, anyway," Caldwell said. "Only luma."

"Also, our facility safety systems would have detected an above-average energy activity," Lancy added. "We closely monitor the energy levels of the crystal at all times for safety purposes, and so the lab team can analyze it. If more energy than what's needed for a test had been released by the crystal, we would have seen it immediately."

"And I suppose that's monitored twenty-four-seven, right?" Novau said.

Lancy nodded. "There's always someone on duty to check the energy levels from their computer, even in the middle of the night. Then, everything's recorded and sent to me and several other teams. Everything was clear the night Isaline died."

So that's it, Reine thought. Someone had poisoned Isaline before she went into the Core Room, and her heart suddenly stopped beating after being overstimulated by copsiamine. But who would want her dead? Could it be Elante, the lab manager, so he could get Isaline's job, or at least get rid of her because of some disagreements, perhaps? But why go to the Core Room to find her body, then? That would immediately draw unwanted attention and make him a potential suspect.

Who else at C3 would wish Isaline dead? Reine barely knew the people working in the company, and didn't feel comfortable making any assumption. What if it was someone outside of work? She didn't know anything about Isaline's personal life. Yet, for some inexplicable reason, she felt like she had known her forever. And now she was gone. All she could do at this point was to cooperate with Novau and help him find the culprit.

Reine was in the security office, reviewing the employee badging logs for the forty-eight hours that preceded the discovery of Isaline's body and checking who went in and out of the labs (and most importantly, where Isaline herself had been before walking into it), when Novau appeared in the doorway.

"Anything interesting?" he asked.

Reine shook her head. "Not really. I reviewed the CCTV recordings of the cafeteria, as well as the corridor leading to Isaline's office, and couldn't find anything interesting. I've still made copies for your team to review, in case I missed something."

Novau grabbed the videotape Reine handed him and said, after thanking her, "I'd like your help with interviewing some employees. Can you join me for the interviews?"

"Suspects?" Reine asked, frowning. Why would Novau ask for her help? She wasn't a police officer.

"Not at this point. I just want to talk to them. And in case you're wondering, which I'm sure you are, I'd appreciate your opinion. Max told me you served at the BCD for almost ten years as a team leader."

Reine raised an eyebrow. "That doesn't make me a detective."

"No, but I trust a former BCD leader to have skills I value for my investigation. Leading a BCD team requires intelligence, grit, and good instincts."

It was true, but Novau's request still surprised her. Reine's job wasn't to solve crimes. It was to prevent them from happening—a job at which she had obviously failed, and even if it wasn't her fault since she had been with C3 for only one day, it was still her responsibility and it made her feel awful.

"I only ask for one hour of your time," Novau said. "Maybe two."

"How many employees are we talking about?"

"Three. They all work in the labs, reporting to Elante."

Reine nodded, grabbed a notebook and pen, and escorted Novau to the labs.

The first person they interviewed was a lab technician named Al Galano. An enmagineer, like most C3 lab employees. Reine sat in a corner of the meeting room they had booked, Galano eyeing her with an inquisitive look that screamed, *what in heavens are we all doing here?* But Reine remained silent and let Novau lead the discussion, chiming in when appropriate. Novau asked Galano what Reine supposed were routine questions, like what his job at C3 was, how he interacted with Isaline, what he knew about her, and what he was doing the night she died.

Galano had nothing interesting or incriminating to share, and at some point, he started sighing noisily and said, "Look, I know you're only doing your job, detective, but I've got nothing to do with it. The less I interacted with

Isaline, the better."

"What do you mean?" Reine blurted. She would have loved to interact more with Isaline, if she'd had the opportunity.

Novau gave Reine a surprised look, but said, too, "Yeah, what do you mean?"

Galano sighed. "She's—*she was a bully*. Udo, my manager, has been doing his best to…shield the team from her."

"Was he in conflict with her?"

"No," Galano said. "She trusted him, and he knew how to…*handle* her, so we—the team—wouldn't have to suffer her outbursts."

Reine had a hard time imagining Isaline being mean or shouting at anybody. Yet she knew how some people could show a different side of their personality depending on who they interacted with. Unless Galano was lying, of course, or perhaps Isaline had just been assertive, and Galano didn't like it.

Anyway, Reine wouldn't decide now if Isaline had been a bad leader or not. It wasn't the time to judge her, because the dead couldn't defend themselves.

"What about you?" Novau asked. "Were you in conflict with her?"

"Like I said, Udo did our best to limit the interactions between Isaline and the team. We rarely worked directly with her."

"But you could have felt resentment for some decisions she made that impacted your work."

Galano sighed again. "Sometimes, but I would have never harmed Isaline. I'm not—I'm not a killer."

Novau raised an eyebrow. "What makes you think she was murdered?"

"Well, that's what Max has been saying, right?"

Novau clicked his tongue, muttered something inaudible, and said, "We are considering foul play, yes."

Reine cleared her throat and asked, "Do you know why Isaline would run three safety tests in a row?" She knew the evidence suggested a copsiamine poisoning, and she was glad Novau's team investigated that lead seriously, but she didn't like how they had ruled out the safety accident altogether. Yes, Isaline had died of sudden cardiac arrest, but the crystal could have caused it, couldn't it? They all kept saying it was safe, but she would always remember Isaline's hesitation. How she pressed her shoulder to keep her away from the crystal. The fear in her eyes. That thing was a pure miracle of technology that enmagineers themselves barely understood, Isaline had admitted. It had been safe so far—for decades—but what if it wasn't anymore? Why run *three* safety tests in the dead of night when she had never done it before? It was her intuition talking, Reine knew, but hadn't Novau said that good instincts were a good thing?

Galano shrugged. "I don't know. I wish you could ask her directly. She surely had her reasons."

"Were you aware of any safety concerns?" Reine continued.

"No. The crystal is safe."

Reine clenched her fists, wondering if learning to repeat that mantra was part of C3's onboarding process, and when she would be subjected to some mandatory training about it.

Having nothing more to ask, Novau thanked Galano for his time and dismissed him. A few minutes after he had left the room, someone knocked on the door.

The woman who walked in had common brown eyes like Reine's, announcing her as one of the few non-enmagineers working in C3's labs. Novau had her introduce herself, allowing Reine to learn that she was named Lou Minati, one of the newest team members, having joined the company for her expertise in electrical engineering despite not being able to work with the crystal directly. The crystal converted luma into energy, which was then used to create electricity, she explained, and if she couldn't work on the earliest stages of the production process, she had no trouble working on the later stages and researching how to improve the electricity supply.

Novau went on with his questions, until Reine interrupted and asked again, causing Novau to frown at her this time, "Do you know why Isaline would run three safety tests in a row?"

Minati's eyes opened wide as if Reine had said something astonishing, and she said, "I can't believe she finally listened."

Novau sighed. "Listened to what?"

"I told her several times that I had concerns about… about…."

"About the crystal's safety?" Reine blurted.

"No, no," Minati said, glancing at Novau with a concerned look. "The crystal is safe."

Reine bit her lips, stifling a sigh. "Then, if it's safe, what did you tell Isaline that led her to run these safety tests?"

Minati didn't respond immediately, visibly taking time to think, then she said, "I noticed some inconsistencies in the energy flow from the crystal. I don't want to bother you with technical stuff, but I"—she lowered her voice—"I've been telling Isaline that she should look at it, check if everything was right. It could have been a faulty cable, too few or too much luma fed to the crystal, or some other parameter…I don't know. I'm not an enmagineer, see?"

"And what did Ms. Caldwell say to your concerns?" Novau asked.

Minati shrugged. "That she's an enmagineer and

knows what she's doing. To stay in my lane, in short."

"Had you told your manager before talking to Isaline?"

Minati gulped. "I—yes. He said he would talk to her, but nothing happened. So, I told Isaline directly. I thought perhaps she would listen if she heard it directly from the team. I showed her some data, but she dismissed me every time I brought the topic up, saying everything was normal in the Core Room." She looked at Novau, then at Reine, and asked, "Did she…did she find anything before…her death?"

"No," Reine said. "She ran three tests, and they all came back perfect."

"Hmm." Minati seemed lost in her thoughts for a moment, then she looked up at Novau quietly, as if awaiting more questions.

But Novau didn't have any, so he thanked her, said he would be in touch if he had any more questions, and let her walk out of the room.

He looked at Reine with an inquisitive gaze, to which Reine responded with, "Is it how you imagined these interviews would go?"

"That's the thing about interviewing witnesses and other persons of interest," Novau said. "You never know what to expect."

Reine was about to ask him what he thought of

Minati's concerns, and what he would do with that information, when the third employee—an enmagineer who looked oddly like Galano, making Reine wonder if they were related—entered the room.

He introduced himself as Sye Avena and sat quietly in front of Novau, but unlike Galano and Minati, he didn't look at ease at all. Not that Galano and Minati seemed to enjoy the experience, and like most people, they would have preferred to avoid talking to a detective under these circumstances, but Avena's body language exuded nervousness. From his fidgeting hands to his tapping foot, along with his sidelong glances, all the man wanted was to leave the room—which he could do anytime, Novau told him. He wasn't a suspect, and he had no obligation to talk to the police.

Avena moved to stand up as Novau said that but hesitated and sat again. Then he said, "I knew this would happen, but nobody listens to me."

This was a serious allegation that Novau immediately picked up. "You knew Ms. Caldwell would die?"

"No, I didn't know *she* would die. I just knew *someone* would die, eventually."

Novau looked underwhelmed but still intrigued. "Die of what?"

"The crystal. We've got no clue how this thing really works and uses the luma we feed it. All we know is that it works, and we're happy with it. We've grown it for forty years, keeping it under control, harvesting its energy, being fortunate enough for the thing to be harmless, but—" He paused, sighed and looked at Reine. Then he continued, a little quieter, "I'm sorry, I shouldn't have said that. I shouldn't let my doubt overcome me. Please don't tell Max I spoke ill of the crystal. I know I should have more faith. It's been a little hard for me at home, and now, Isaline is gone...."

Reine didn't know how to respond. Did Avena fear her? Did he worry she would go straight to Max Caldwell to tell him how an employee didn't believe the crystal to be safe? This wasn't why she had been hired. Her role was to protect employees, not report their dissent opinion on scientific matters to their boss.

"Do you have any reason to doubt the crystal's safety?" Reine asked.

"No," Avena said, standing up to leave. "I have nothing more to say."

Novau thanked Reine for her time and said he would debrief with her the next day.

"I would love to do it now," he said as he shook Reine's hand, "but I need to get back home as soon as possible if I don't want my wife and kids and pets to kill me."

Reine could well imagine how a high-profile investigation like this one kept Novau away from his family, so she nodded and waved him goodbye.

She went back to the security office and sat down in front of the CCTV monitors. One of her team members stood up and left the office for a round, and she realized with shame that she wasn't sure if his name was Orlan or Orson. She had been so distracted by Isaline's death and the hectic last days that she'd barely taken the time to get to know her team. To think she would take the greatest pride in knowing each member of her team at the BCD! She hadn't been with C3 for a week and she was already a bad security lead and a worse manager.

She cursed under her breath, not wanting to add *rude* to the list of complaints people could have against her, and looked at the CCTV monitors absentmindedly.

Reine saw nothing unusual until she noticed Novau hadn't left the building. She frowned and got closer to the monitor. Novau was exiting the elevator on the twenty-ninth floor and walking to Max Caldwell's office. He entered immediately after knocking.

There was no camera inside Caldwell's office, of course, and Reine could only assume that Novau had something important to tell him that couldn't wait for a phone call.

Bright City, Shattered

When the office door opened again, Caldwell walked outside of his office with Novau. There wasn't any audio coming from the CCTV, and the image quality wasn't good enough that Reine could read lips to guess what they said, so she didn't know what the two men were talking about (the investigation, she supposed) but she couldn't help but notice how they both seemed satisfied—almost *cheerful*—and hugged each other like old friends before parting.

The place Reine had found for her family was a two-bedroom apartment in the middle of the Big District. Not the best place to live in, but not the worst either, and Mama and Nola were happy enough with it.

Papa had been back from the hospital for a week now, and losing a limb seemed to affect him less than losing the house. He hated living on the fourth floor of a building and wished he were lying down on a beach towel, enjoying the fresh sea breeze, instead of the recliner he sat in while he dressed his stump with Mama's help.

"We can't even see the ocean from here," he mumbled as Mama took the used medical supplies away.

"You know the upper floors are in high demand," Reine said. "There wasn't anything available above the sixth floor."

The higher the floor, the more expensive the rent; it was the same in every district. Even the south-facing apartments with no view of the ocean were in high demand, as people enjoyed the opportunity to gaze at a horizon they would probably never reach. It made them feel less trapped, because the city felt like a cage. A golden cage, but a cage nonetheless. The gates were always open, and nobody forced to stay, but only a fool would leave Bright City. Living in a beach house beyond the wall was the most dangerous thing people would consider doing, and pearl divers often paid a high price for it, like Papa did. Leaving the city had a price nobody wanted to pay.

"At least you don't get too much light from the crystal," Reine said. "It can be a little annoying during nighttime."

"Bah, we'd just install some proper shutters," Papa said.

Reine had no answer, so she remained silent.

"Talking about the crystal," Mama said as she came back to the living room, "how are things going at work with the ongoing investigation?"

Reine exhaled, thinking about the awkwardness of interviewing people alongside Novau. "I helped Detective Inspector Novau interview some employees today."

Mama raised an eyebrow. "I didn't realize you were so deeply involved in the investigation."

Deeply wasn't how Reine thought she was involved. *Weirdly* sounded more appropriate.

"That poor woman," Mama continued. "She was so young. Not even forty."

"Is it true what the newspapers say?" Nola asked, shouting from her bedroom. "That the police—"

"Stop doing that," Mama shouted back, "and come with us in the living room." She turned to Reine and shook her head, whispering, "It's so annoying when she does that."

Nola appeared in the doorframe. "Is it true that Isaline Caldwell was murdered?"

Reine gave her a tense smile that meant *I'm not supposed to tell you more*, but still said, "It's one lead the police are investigating."

"How captivating," Nola said, her eyes opening wide. "My sister is part of a murder investigation."

Reine clicked her tongue. "We don't know if it's a murder for sure—"

"Not yet," Nola interrupted.

She's read too many books, Reine thought, slowly shaking her head while looking at Nola. When Nola wasn't coding in her room for some school project, she was lost in *Noir Light*, her weekly murder mystery magazine.

"Don't be so excited, young lady," Mama said, visibly thinking alike. "A woman died, and there's no reason to be thrilled about it."

"I'm not thrilled someone died," Nola said, lowering her voice. "I just hope they catch the culprit soon."

"Like I said," Reine continued, "we don't know the cause yet. It could be an accident, or something else." She couldn't imagine Isaline overdosing voluntarily on her copsiamine treatment, and Max Caldwell sounded adamant that she wouldn't do it, but it was still a possibility. But why spend the night in the Core Room after ingesting high doses of copsiamine, running test after test? Wouldn't she want to be home if she were taking her own life? Reine didn't know, and perhaps she was wrong. She was no more a psychiatrist than she was an investigator. Nothing in Isaline's death made sense, anyway. Yet, the truth had to be exposed. Regardless of what had caused Isaline's death, she had to know. The city had to know. And if someone had caused her death, they would be brought to justice, should it be for murder or gross negligence.

"What do *you* think?" Mama asked.

"I don't know," Reine answered, truthfully.

Papa looked her in the eye and asked, "What do your guts tell you?"

Reine took a minute to think. She knew what her guts were telling her, but it sounded bad. Too bad. Still, she said, "I don't know why Isaline died, but I think Max Caldwell is looking for a scapegoat."

Bright City, Shattered

For an instant, Reine wondered if *she* could become the scapegoat.

The next day, Novau called Reine around midday, an hour before their expected meeting time in C3's lobby.

"Can I ask you a favor?" he said.

Reine wasn't in the mood to do anyone a favor, but still answered, "What will it be, detective?"

"Would you meet me at the police station? I'm swamped with paperwork and would appreciate some time to complete my work and have lunch instead of being stuck in traffic driving to C3."

Traffic was always bad in Bright City. There was no downtime, even at night. During the rush hour, it simply went from *bad* to *worse,* and the subway wasn't better, going from *packed* to *jam-packed.*

Reine wasn't eager to hop into a taxi and skip her own lunch so she could arrive at the police station in time, but Novau graciously said, "I'll get us some sandwiches. That work for you?"

"Hold on a minute."

She covered the mouthpiece with her right hand and told the team members present in the office—*Orlan* and *Maia,* that was—she would be away for a couple of hours to debrief with Novau. After they answered with unconcerned nods, she told Novau she was on her way and left.

Novau had picked up sandwiches from Dan's Deli. It appeared to be the lunch place of choice for police officers, considering the number of them Reine saw eating Dan's Deli sandwiches as Novau escorted her to his office.

"I got you a Beach Boy," he said, sitting down at his desk. "Sounded appropriate considering you grew up in a beach house and you…well—"

"Look like a guy?" she said, looking him in the eye with a half-amused, half-irritated look.

Novau had a nervous laugh. "People must have told you, am I right?"

Reine clicked her tongue and admitted, "Yes." She didn't like the way Novau had brought up the topic, but it was true that some people mistook her for a man or stared at her with a confused look, unsure of how to address her. She didn't care about it—as long as people weren't rude.

"See? I knew I'd picked the right sandwich. It's a rainbow tuna sandwich. You like seafood, don't you?"

Reine didn't like people assuming her likes or tastes either, but Novau was right: she *loved* seafood. So she nodded, thanked him, and ate the sandwich.

"So, what was your impression?" Novau asked, taking a pack of cigarettes from his jacket's inner pocket.

"I'm not a detective, so take my impression with a grain of salt, but I don't think any of them have anything to do with what happened to Isaline," Reine said. "That is basing my judgment on the interviews only, of course."

Novau lit the cigarette. "What about Al Galano?"

"He's not the first to dislike his boss, and he won't be the last."

"Yeah," Novau said. "True. What about the other guy…Sye Avena. He was nervous as heck and barely answered any questions after saying that he knew this would happen. Do you think I should task my team with investigating him more?"

"I agree about the nervousness, but I think it's because of his safety concerns. I know everybody believes the crystal is safe—"

"It *is* safe. Even Ms. Caldwell's tests came back perfect."

Reine stifled a sigh. She didn't pursue the matter and remained silent. She had nothing more to share about Avena. If Novau wanted to talk to him again or investigate him more, it was his job to decide, but Reine had no reason to suspect him—or anyone else. He knew something, Reine was sure, but it was about the crystal's safety, and nobody seemed interested in listening to that. Even Avena himself had eventually been unwilling to share more.

Novau finally asked, "And what about the woman… Lou Minati?"

"She also voiced some concerns about the crystal, but nothing she said made me think she would harm Isaline."

"I think I'm going to have the team look into her a bit more," Novau continued, as if he hadn't listened to a single thing Reine had just said.

"Why?"

"She joined the team a few months ago and right away, she challenged Ms. Caldwell's work. I also learned, thanks to your boss, that she had applied for an internship position in Ms. Caldwell's team but was rejected because she was only hiring enmagineers for that position. When the recruiter called her back to share the bad news, Ms. Minati went on a rant saying Ms. Caldwell was, I quote, 'a spoiled brat who only got her job because her uncle runs the company.' She later apologized, saying it was inappropriate and just the frustration talking, but that's still a red flag to me."

"And you think she wanted to get revenge on Isaline for refusing her an internship? By *murdering* her?"

"I know it sounds crazy, but there are some really crazy people in the city, you know."

Reine shook her head. "If all she wanted was to work at C3, she got it. Why get revenge on something as trivial as an internship? She got *an actual job*. Which, by the way, seems odd considering what she said about Isaline."

"Mr. Caldwell agreed to hire her because he's a good man who believes in second chances. He's regretting it now." Novau stubbed out his cigarette. "I truly appreciate your cooperation, Reine. You've been very helpful, and I think I'm now able to move the investigation forward."

Reine didn't take a taxi back to C3. She wanted to walk. She wanted to think.

The debrief with Novau had been a joke. A formality, something Novau did to check a box to complete his investigation. He had never been interested in Reine's opinion, had he? Not that Reine had anything helpful to share about the three interviewees, but Novau didn't seem interested in listening, anyway. Then, why invite her to the interviews in the first place? Was it all for show?

Reine didn't know, and perhaps it was for the best. She had never asked to be involved in the investigation. Of course, she wanted to help find what happened to Isaline, and had shared all the information and recordings she had with Novau, but she wasn't qualified for *more*. She wanted to let the police do their job, and establish herself as the security lead at C3 so there wouldn't be the need for investigations anymore. It was all she could do.

This was, at least, what she thought as she walked through the crowded streets of the Newtown District, trying to ignore the flashing neon lights catching her eyes despite the broad daylight.

After walking for ten minutes toward the Inner Sunrise, the district where the C3 Tower was located, Reine stopped at an information board displaying a map of the area. Finding the C3 Tower was easy; she just had to look up and follow the light. Still, the maze-like streets were trickier to navigate than they looked.

She felt the passersby's curious glances on her back as she scrutinized the map. Nobody ever looked at the maps. An outsider, they probably thought—which she was, admittedly. She had spent all her life on the edges of the city and was still learning to navigate its center.

A voice rising from the crowd distracted her from the map. She turned her head to find its origin, but all she could see was the uninterrupted flow of people coming and going and glancing at her. The voice grew louder, and soon the glances turned to it and Reine saw a man trying to stir up the crowd, shouting some unintelligible tirade. Two passersby stopped to listen to him, and Reine approached, too.

"…is going to kill us all, for we have sinned by stealing nature's most precious resource! Have you ever wondered why beasts are trying to kill us every time we step outside the city? It's because we're stealing their precious luma."

Bullshit, Reine thought. Whistling whales and razor-toothed wolves and giant bears had always been a problem for the city's safety, long before enmagineering allowed Bright City to transition to luma-powered electricity. Her own family had suffered attacks from whistling whales for generations, and the tales of assaults and lost limbs haunted her childhood memories.

But…attacks were becoming more frequent, too. The forest was already dangerous and its beasts lethal when Reine joined the BCD, but it had grown deadlier year after year. The ambush that had almost killed Reine's men would have been unthinkable ten years ago, yet it had become a reality—and a common one now, Reine had learned from her former colleagues. There was some truth in what the man said, but Reine couldn't see why he blamed it on the city's use of luma. Luma was plentiful, and enmagineers never lacked work. It was like saying Bright City's citizens were starving the forest of oxygen by breathing too much air.

"Now it's coming for us," the man continued as one passerby shrugged and left. "Isaline Caldwell is the first to die for our sins."

"What in heavens?" Reine blurted.

"Don't you watch the news?" the remaining passerby

asked her.

Reine wished she'd had time to snap back at the man, but he'd left before Reine could answer. Instead, she let out a long, exhausted sigh. She didn't need to watch the news to know Isaline was dead.

Ignoring the continuing rant from the doomsday preacher, she turned around and continued her route back to the C3 Tower. It took her through the busier-than-busy Altercity District where immigrants from other cities lived, most of whom had come by sea from other, poorer coastal cities. Some came from the inner cities, driving their fast, light cars through the forest, but few people ever reached Bright City that way. During her time at the BCD, Reine had seen at least a dozen abandoned car wrecks covered in vegetation, their metal lacerated by claws belonging to giant bears, and sometimes she even saw the mutilated corpses of their owners, making her squeeze her power gun.

A teenage newsboy who looked like he came from a southern coastal city shouted vague but sensational headlines to the passersby. Reine hadn't read the paper or watched the news since Isaline's death, and had been evading the relentless journalists standing next to C3's entrance for that long. She grabbed a coin from her pocket and purchased a copy of what happened to be the *Daily Light*, the city's most popular newspaper, printed on over-recycled paper. It was time to see how the press covered the affair.

Unsurprisingly, the front page didn't cover the investigation. Everything went fast in the city, and Isaline's death was already old news. Unless a breakthrough happened—a suspect arrested or a revelation—the *Daily Light* would relegate the investigation to the second page, if not the following ones.

Reine unfolded the newspaper and opened it to the second page. She found a long article about the investigation's progress that Reine scanned briefly until her eyes got caught by a subhead that read: "Employee raises work ethics and safety concerns."

She read the article as fast as she could. Her eyes widened, all her suspicions coming back at once. The *Daily Light* wasn't one of these tabloids always looking for some juicy scandal, willing to distort reality to sell more copies. It was a serious, respected daily. If they had published an article, it was only because they judged the source reliable. Reine wondered who had spoken to the paper's journalists. Avena, Minati, or someone else?

She folded the newspaper and ran toward the C3 Tower.

"Max is unavailable at this time," Allie said, leaning on her elbows while flipping through the electronic pages of her personal digital assistant. "He's in a meeting with the deputy mayor until two-thirty."

Reine considered ignoring what Allie had said, and imagined herself walking to the elevator, pressing the "29" button, and walking straight to Max Caldwell's office, ignoring her boss's protests as she opened the door and interrupted what must have been a high-priority meeting. It made her smirk, but she didn't act on that impulse. She thanked Allie and walked to the elevator, where she did press the "29" button, but instead of rushing to Caldwell's office and pushing the door open, resigned herself to wait in the hallway.

During the twenty-something minutes her wait lasted, Reine re-read the *Daily Light* article three times. It was terse, as if the journalist worried about disclosing too many details. The journalist did question the safety of enmagineers' work at C3 and dared to ask if Isaline's death was accidental. The article didn't mention Pabst's disease, though. It ended with a question Reine didn't have an answer to: "If C3 is not safe for its own people and must close its doors, how can we power our city without going back to the Smog Age?"

At 2:30, the office door opened. The deputy mayor and Max Caldwell appeared in the hallway and shook hands, not paying attention to Reine's presence.

"Mr. Caldwell, I truly appreciate your commitment to

Bright City," the deputy mayor said.

Caldwell smiled. "Always."

The deputy mayor eventually glanced at Reine and gave her a polite smile to acknowledge her presence. The deputy mayor was the second most important elected official in Bright City after the mayor-president. She was a tall woman who had come from an inner city forty years ago, right when Florence Caldwell founded C3, and had made a name for herself in politics despite not being a native citizen of the city-state. Rumors said she came from a place called Dark City, but nobody knew for sure such a place existed, and Reine herself thought it was just a hoax spread by political opponents who lacked imagination.

Once the deputy mayor reached the elevator and disappeared from the twenty-ninth floor, Caldwell looked at Reine and said, gesturing to invite her inside his office, "You've come at the right time."

It was true indeed, but Reine didn't think Caldwell shared the same reasons for wanting to talk. She followed him inside the office and sat in one of the two guest chairs—the same one she used three weeks ago when he offered her the job and when the wave hit the city.

"Mr. Caldwell," Reine started.

"I've already told you, Reine. Call me Max."

"*Max*," she said, still uneasy about calling him by his first name. "I'm concerned about the direction the investigation is taking."

"Are you?" he said, raising an eyebrow. "I've had a chat with Detective Inspector Novau over the phone after lunch, and we both agreed the investigation was moving much faster than we expected."

Reine put the newspaper on the desk, opened to the second page. "Aren't we eliminating some leads too hastily?"

Caldwell barely looked at the newspaper and said, clasping his hand, "So, you've seen it."

"Yes, and I suppose the rest of the city will soon have read it, and that it will be on the news tonight."

"Oh no, I assure you it won't." He sounded certain of himself.

Reine frowned. "How do you know?"

"Because whoever wrote that article did a poor job verifying its sources, and I made sure to let our TV anchors know. The crystal is safe. C3 is safe. All our test results can attest to it. I'm willing to release them to the press if needed."

Reine had a hard time understanding him. Was he honest, doing his best to defend the company's reputation, unfairly attacked? Or was he trying to silence whistleblowers and pressuring the press not to give them a platform? Max Caldwell had such power, Reine suspected. He led the only company producing electricity in the entire city. If he wanted to control what was being said in a television studio, he could threaten to flip the switch and deprive the TV channel of its single source of power.

"How do you know the sources aren't reliable?" she asked.

Reine was still willing to give him the benefit of the doubt until he responded, "We know who talked to the press, and C3 terminated her this morning."

"Her?"

"Lou Minati. I suspected that she'd been disclosing trade secrets to the press for several weeks now. Emyr gave her a termination letter this morning, and that guy from your team, Orlan, escorted her out of the office about an hour ago. I was planning to ask you to escort her, but your team told me you were having lunch with Novau."

A strange feeling seized Reine. How convenient for Novau to call her to the police headquarters when Minati was being escorted out of C3, so she wouldn't question the decision and interfere. Was it all agreed between Max Caldwell and Novau? Did they fear that her lack of enthusiasm for the murder scenario would make her unwilling to execute a direct order? Reine sighed, and wondered: if she had been here, would she have complied? Would have she escorted Minati out like a criminal? She didn't know, and it worried her for too many reasons. She had never disobeyed a direct order from a superior. Ten years in the

BCD made you respectful of hierarchy, so she couldn't see herself challenging Caldwell. But she never had a reason to disobey an order at the BCD. Her superiors always treated her and her unit fairly and never assigned them unrealistic missions. Even if serving in the BCD was dangerous by nature, they had the safety of the BCD personnel at heart. Did Max Caldwell have the safety of C3's employees at heart? Did he have the safety *of his own niece* at heart?

Reine asked, "Were her concerns really illegitimate?"

Caldwell opened his mouth to respond but remained silent. He pouted, then finally said, very quietly, almost whispering, "Listen, Reine. If you don't believe in this company, no one's forcing you to stay. I hired you because you came with great recommendations from your former superiors, and I expected you to know how to differentiate between hard-working, loyal employees, and the incompetent ones."

Reine did her best not to open her eyes wide and frown at what he said. She didn't even know where to start her response—if he expected a response at all. Reine wasn't familiar with office politics, but she suspected it was one of these moments where your boss asked for your blind allegiance, or to stand down and leave.

Neither of the two options appealed to her, so she diverted the conversation. "Don't doubt that I have the best interests of C3 at heart, Max," she said. "I know our technology is essential to the city, and that you too, most of all, care about the company. It's in the company's interest to ensure C3 is safe and to investigate employees' concerns—as unlikely as they may be. Terminating an employee who was speaking out in good faith will only raise suspicion that we're hiding something."

"In good faith?" Caldwell said, his voice becoming louder. "She was leaking trade secrets to the press, for heavens' sake!"

Reine couldn't believe it. Nothing in the *Daily Light* article mentioned confidential information about C3's technology.

"Still—"

"I don't have time for that," Caldwell snapped. "If you truly have the company's best interest at heart, let the police do their job. Stay in your lane, Reine. You've done your part. Do the job I hired you to do."

He gave her a look that obviously meant *don't make me regret I hired you*, and Reine knew that if she wanted to keep her job, the conversation was over.

Caldwell looked like he was indeed done talking, but as Reine moved to stand up and leave, he said, "You weren't in the office when I needed you to escort Minati out, but you're here now. Go clean up her office. I want it available right away for another employee to use. Collect her belongings into a box and bring it to my office."

Reine clenched her fists, using every bit of self-control she still had not to react to the humiliation Caldwell imposed on her.

She nodded, took the newspaper, and left.

Reine wasn't the type to balk at executing tasks below her pay grade, but what Max Caldwell had asked her was only meant as a punishment for daring to criticize Minati's termination. She couldn't see another reason for asking her to clean up an office—Minati's, no less. Caldwell hadn't said the words, but Reine wasn't stupid. *You didn't want me to fire her? Well, now you're going to clean up her mess, and next time you'll keep your mouth shut.* That's what his request meant to say.

She still executed it, not ready to dive into the muddy waters of insubordination. *Not yet,* she told herself as she walked into Minati's office.

There wasn't much to clean up. Minati had been with C3 for only a few months and hadn't had the time to accumulate office supplies and gadgets and certificates to pin onto the walls like others had. A picture of Minati holding a young boy that must have been her son still stood next to the monitor, convincing Reine than Minati hadn't had the time to collect *anything* before being escorted out. Exhaling, she collected what appeared to belong to Minati in a first box: the picture, some snacks she found in a drawer, an underwatered plant, and a jacket still hanging on the door hook.

Next were Minati's work files and devices, that all belonged to C3. Her computer—a thick, heavy, but portable device—was still connected to the large monitor on the desk. Reine unplugged the cables and put the computer in a box she labeled as C3's materials. She left the pens, paper clips, stapler, and other office supplies on the desk, assuming the next occupant would need them. Then she opened each drawer to look for binders, folders, and other documents, scanning everything she found to confirm if it was indeed C3's proprietary materials, or personal documents that should be returned to Minati.

Two piles of folders already covered the computer in the C3 box when Reine came across what looked like Minati's medical records. At first, she closed the folder right after scanning the first page, and placed it in the box with Minati's belongings, but something caught her attention. She reopened the folder and reread the first page. It was a form Minati had filled out when visiting Lancy to get pain killers for migraine that included basic health information, and a question that read *Do you have any known allergies to medications?* Minati had responded with the following answer, that made Reine freeze as she read it: *Yes. Severe allergic reactions to naproxen, diazepam, and copsiamine.*

So, Minati was allergic to copsiamine.

Reine kept reading, learning that Minati suffered not only from migraines but also from epilepsy. She must have tried copsiamine as a treatment for epilepsy, Reine guessed. Lancy had said the drug helped regulate the body's electric currents, and abnormal electrical brain activity caused epilepsy.

She took a moment to consider the information.

Max Caldwell and Detective Inspector Novau were chasing the copsiamine poisoning lead like a razor-toothed wolf with a bone. Novau wanted to investigate Minati further. She was the only non-enmagineer in the lab team, making her…expendable. And now, Caldwell had fired her from C3. *The perfect scapegoat,* Reine thought. Except Minati couldn't poison Isaline with a substance she was severely allergic to, unless she was ready to risk her own life manipulating it. She would also have to get it illegally, since no physician would prescribe her a drug that would kill her. That seemed like an unlikely and dangerous way to murder someone to get revenge for something as trivial as not getting an internship.

Maybe Caldwell didn't know about her allergy, if Lancy had kept the information private as she should have. Maybe he didn't realize Minati wasn't the perfect scapegoat, after all. Maybe he was feeding her to the wolves, not realizing they would swallow her whole only to regurgitate her when they'd realize she wasn't edible.

Reine didn't put the folder back into the box. Instead, she folded it, put it in the inside pocket of her jacket, and kept sorting out documents, her heart beating as fast as the day she and her unit had run from a pack of deadly wolves.

After dropping the two boxes into Caldwell's office, Reine went to the security office and asked her team to leave her alone and go on their afternoon rounds. They didn't question the request, but the look on their faces betrayed how worried they were. Perhaps her own face looked worried, too, Reine supposed…because she definitely was.

Once they were gone, she sat in front of the CCTV monitors and went back to the recordings of the morning Isaline's body had been discovered in the Core Room. She played the scenes again. The recording of Elante finding Isaline's body inside the Core Room. Elante walking into Caldwell's office. Caldwell running to the Core Room and finding Isaline's body. Elante going to Lancy's office, hoping she would be there and perform first aid. She watched them again. Isaline's body discovered. Caldwell's office. Lancy's office. Again. Isaline's body. Caldwell's office. Lancy's office. And again. Isaline. Caldwell. Lancy.

She played the scenes three more times, wondering what she actually looked for, what she had missed.

Isaline. Caldwell. Lancy. Isaline. Caldwell. Lancy. Isaline. Caldwell. Lancy.

After watching the recordings so many times, they didn't make sense anymore, and Reine was about to stop playing the videos when she noticed something. At first, she thought it was her mind playing tricks on her from watching the same images over and over, but when she played the video again, she realized it wasn't her mind at all.

A full minute of video was missing in the recording showing Elante walking into Max Caldwell's office. How could have she missed it? Because it wasn't easily noticeable, she thought as she replayed the video. The camera only showed Caldwell's office door closed, recording nothing else of interest, but the time displayed in tiny captions in the lower part of the screen went from 7:45:59 to 7:47:00 instead of 7:46:00. Someone had cut the recording methodically, removing exactly one minute of footage. It couldn't be a malfunction of the camera; such a perfect minute would be too big of a coincidence. It had been done intentionally, with the hope that no one would notice—and it had almost worked. But why? Did Caldwell and Elante leave the office and didn't want to be seen? Reine looked at the recording of other cameras in the vicinity, and at the one facing the elevator to check they hadn't been to another floor, but couldn't see them from 7:46:00 to 7:47:00. It seemed they had stayed in the office for that entire minute. Why cut the recording, then? And what if it was, after all, a genuine, oddly timed technical error?

She looked back at the video of Elante finding Isaline's body, squinting at the screen to check the time displayed on the screen for another anomaly, but everything looked fine. Then she looked at the video showing Caldwell running to Isaline's body. Same. The timer was normal; nothing was missing. Finally, she watched again the video of Elante running to Lancy's office, and—there, again! Two full minutes were missing this time. Not consecutive, though. The timer went from 7:48:59 to 7:50:00, then from 7:50:59 to 7:52:00. Similarly, it was when the video only showed Lancy's office door closed. Reine rewatched the recordings of the cameras in the vicinity, and couldn't see Elante going anywhere. He had, too, stayed in Lancy's office for these two full minutes.

She leaned back in her seat. Why would Max Caldwell want to remove three minutes of recording of him and Elante behind closed office doors? Because it was him, of course. Only Caldwell—or Reine herself—could have tampered with the recordings. He was the only person besides her who had full access to the CCTV. Caldwell had access to *everything* at C3. Nothing was off-limits to him—the CCTV, the labs, the Core Room, the computers...he even received the safety test reports, Lancy had told Reine.

The safety test reports, Reine almost shouted. These three better-than-normal, perfect reports.

Four people at C3 received the reports. Four people who got a copy on their computer. Isaline, Caldwell, Elante, *and Lancy.*

Reine quickly made a copy of the troubling CCTV recordings, put the cassette in her pocket, and left the security office.

It was time to talk with Elante.

Reine didn't announce herself when she walked into Elante's office. Elante was a tall slender man in his fifties who looked like he had never experienced a joyful day in his life, and Reine wasn't about to change that.

Elante frowned at her and asked, with a half-hesitant, half-annoyed voice, "Can I help you, Reine?"

"Did you tamper with the safety test reports?" Reine simply asked, looking Elante in the eye.

Elante lifted an eyebrow, but he also gulped and Reine noticed it. "What are you talking about?"

"The three tests Isaline ran before you found her dead in the Core Room. Did you tamper with the reports?"

Elante clasped his hands and said, slowly shaking his

head, "I did not, and I have no idea why you are throwing such a ridiculous accusation at me."

Reine had seen many people lying, some so good at it that they had fooled her several times before she caught them, but Elante wasn't one of them. The way he looked Reine in the eye and tried to sound so assured…he was trying to convince himself as much as he was trying to convince Reine. "Why did you go to Lancy's office after reporting Isaline's death to Max Caldwell?"

Elante gulped again, and said very quickly, with a flat voice, "Because I didn't know for sure if Isaline was dead and wanted to get Araya's help. She's a nurse."

"Oh, and that's why you stayed more than three minutes in her office after you realized she wasn't there, right?" Reine said, with a sarcastic tone she didn't know she could have. "Did you open all her desk's drawers to check she wasn't hiding in there?" *You could have just given Lancy a phone call from Max Caldwell's office, too,* Reine thought but didn't say.

He opened his mouth to respond, but remained silent, as if in shock. At last, he said, "I checked if she wasn't in the medical supply room adjacent to her office, then I left as soon as I realized she wasn't there. I didn't stay for what you say…more than three minutes. Also, there's no need to be so rude."

Reine snorted at his sloppy excuse. Even so, checking

the room adjacent to Lancy's office wouldn't have taken long. "I'm rude, and you're a liar—a pretty bad one, on top of that. Tell me, Max asked you after you found Isaline, didn't he? You knew she was dead. There was nothing you could do. So you two checked the test reports together in his office and you found something suspicious, and he asked you to delete it. But you couldn't, because Lancy would have noticed a discrepancy between the energy levels during the night and the number of reports, and could have reported it to the city. You couldn't tamper with the energy level report either—too many people receive it. So instead, you rushed to Lancy's office, used a backdoor password that Max gave you to access her computer—I'd be surprised if he doesn't have one—and you edited the safety test reports so she wouldn't see anything unusual. That's why they were *so perfect*, right? I'm sure you did the same on Max's computer and yours, but you couldn't do it on Isaline's computer without looking suspicious." Reine thought about that scene she witnessed live on the CCTV, of Max Caldwell and Novau hugging each other with satisfied looks on their faces, and she added, "I wonder how much Max bribed Novau so he wouldn't get Isaline's computer analyzed."

Reine had never talked to someone like that. She was accusing Elante of conspiring with Max Caldwell to tamper with evidence, looking him right in the eye, and all she had to support it were these three minutes of missing recordings. But it was the only explanation that made sense. It all clicked together. Caldwell had removed these three minutes methodically so nobody would notice how long he and Elante had stayed in the two offices. Reine suspected the first minute was to cover for their time looking at the safety test reports on Caldwell's computer and coming up with a plan, and the two other minutes were for Elante tampering with the reports on Lancy's computer.

"You don't know what you're talking about," Elante said after a moment of awkward silence.

"Maybe *you* know, then."

"Don't play that game, Reine," Elante continued, his voice shifting to a slightly menacing tone Reine didn't fail to notice. "You're still young and have a promising future at C3. You're naive if you believe you'll fulfill it by throwing accusations at everybody."

"I'm not throwing accusations at everybody. Only at you."

"Then you're even more naive than I thought."

Reine shrugged. "Who said I care about having a promising future in this company, anyway?" she said, barely believing she was saying it. But it was true. She had been immensely grateful to Max Caldwell for hiring her, but that was before Isaline died and her own uncle tried to hide evidence that would damage the company's reputation.

"I'm sure Max will be disappointed to hear that."

"That'll make two of us disappointed, then."

And with that, Reine left Elante's office.

Reine left work early. She walked to an electronic store on Grand Avenue in the Inner Sunrise, close to her apartment.

The place was small and dimly lit by a couple of lightbulbs hanging from a dirty drop ceiling. All sorts of products were displayed on the shelves, from keyboard and computer parts to speakers and consoles. A thick layer of dust covered some boxes, while others were still glossy and spotless. The clerk was a short woman in her fifties—probably the owner, Reine guessed—and she was already talking with another customer, a woman asking her about the newest portable computer made by Cygna, the city's main electronic manufacturer.

"The Cygna D is five hundred," the clerk said.

"Could you sell it for four hundred?"

The clerk raised an eyebrow and said, "I can't go that low, my dear. But because you're a regular, I can make a special discount and lower the price to four hundred seventy-five."

"Four hundred and fifty and I take it."

The clerk sighed. "Deal, but I want two hundred upfront."

"When will you get it?" the customer asked, taking two blue bills out of her wallet.

The clerk typed loudly on the keyboard in front of her, squinting at the screen and pushing her glasses up, then she said, "Next week. Come back with the rest of the money and it's yours." She clicked on her mouse and a small printer turned on, slowly printing a document that the clerk handed to the customer as soon as it was ready. "Your order confirmation. Don't lose it."

The customer thanked the clerk, folded the document and put it in her purse, then left the store, glancing at Reine on her way out, a brief, polite smile on her face.

"How can I help you?" the clerk asked, looking at her screen.

"I need a tape recorder."

The clerk cleared her throat. "What model would you like? I've got a C-300 or a C-400."

"A C-300 will be fine."

"It's forty."

It was overpriced, but Reine wasn't in the mood for negotiation—she was bad at it, anyway—so she paid without arguing and left the store right after the clerk handed her the tape recorder, plus a pack of batteries and a couple of cassettes.

She rushed home, weaving her way through the crowd to her building, and impatiently pushed the call button in the lobby. Her hands shook as she closed her apartment door behind her and took the tape recorder out of its box.

She placed the tape recorder on the only table she owned, next to the black phone she bought shortly after moving in, and that had been only used to receive calls from Mama and Max Caldwell so far. Reine was about to place her first call on the new phone, and she wanted to record it. A good thing she had paid extra for a model that had a speakerphone.

Reine wanted to call Novau. She had already lost confidence in Caldwell and needed to confirm her suspicions that Novau was also compromised. The faint hope that she was wrong still hung in the back of her mind, though. She had to be certain, and if she was right, she had to collect evidence. What she would do with the evidence, she didn't know, but it didn't matter yet. She'd think about it later.

She put a cassette inside the tape recorder and tested the device, recording herself. The sound of her own voice came clearly as she played the cassette. She was ready.

Her hands shaking again, Reine dialed Novau's office number and started the recorder as the ringing tone echoed in her studio.

"Detective Inspector Novau?" Reine asked after she heard a hoarse male voice grumble a sharp *yes*. "This is

Reine from C3."

"Ha, Reine. I don't have much time. What's going on? Don't tell me the sandwich made you sick too."

"Sick? No, no, I'm fine."

"Good, because my stomach has been killing me since our lunch. I can't handle spicy food. My wife's been telling me to stop eating that spicy chicken sandwich, but I'm too stubborn to listen. The thing is just too damn good."

"I'm sorry to hear you've got stomach cramps," Reine said politely. She inhaled deeply and continued, "I'm calling about the investigation."

"Oh yes, what about it? We're almost done, thanks to everyone's cooperation, including yours."

"I've discovered something strange about the CCTV recordings."

"And what is it?" Novau said, sounding impatient but not eager to know the answer.

Reine explained how three minutes were missing, and how she suspected Caldwell had edited the recordings so nobody would question why he and Elante had spent so much time in his and Lancy's offices.

"We already have a suspect," Novau interrupted, "and one with a motive. We interviewed your boss and Udo Elante already, and we've got no reason to believe they caused harm to Ms. Caldwell."

"And I agree with that," Reine said very fast before

Novau could continue. "I'm not saying Max or Elante hurt Isaline. What I'm saying is, I believe Max and Elante saw these test reports and they didn't look good at all, so they tampered with the reports so nobody would find out that Isaline's death was caused by a malfunction of the crystal."

Novau laughed. It was a mocking yet uncomfortable laugh that sounded forced. "You've got a wild imagination. I wouldn't have thought that of you."

"Why would Max have removed three entire minutes from the recording?" Reine argued.

"That's what *you're* saying. My team analyzed the recordings that you shared with us and they would've noticed."

Perhaps they hadn't noticed, Reine thought, since she had herself seen it only after watching the recordings several times, but Novau could also be lying. Still, she didn't argue, not bold enough to call a police officer a liar.

"Also," Novau continued, "it could be a malfunction. And if it isn't, why would it be necessarily Mr. Caldwell who did it? Why not someone in your team? Why not *you*, Reine?"

"I want to know what happened to Isaline," Reine almost shouted. "If she's truly been murdered, then so be it! But I don't want someone to go to jail if they've done nothing while we don't address a deadly safety issue that could kill more people! How hard is it to understand?"

"Calm down, Reine. You're a nice person and I've enjoyed meeting you, but you're crossing the line right now. Anyhow, even if I get my guys to look at the recordings again and they find whatever you pretend you've seen, it wouldn't prove anything. I trust hard evidence—the toxicology report that shows a copsiamine poisoning. Not hare-brained ideas coming from someone who's not even a detective."

"Look at the report on Isaline's computer, at the very least. Have it analyzed by a luma expert."

"I'll do my job as I see fit," Novau snapped. "I think we're done. I've got work to do, and so do you."

"Yes," Reine said, bitter. "We're done."

Reine had never been so angry. She, who was always so composed, was now going through emotions she couldn't control. Nola noticed it first when Reine walked into Mama and Papa's apartment, because she asked, eyebrows furrowed in concern, "What's going on?"

Reine didn't respond. She didn't know what to say, so instead she hugged Nola quietly. She couldn't remember the last time she had hugged someone, and Nola was so surprised by the unexpected gesture that she took a moment to react and hug her back.

Papa was watching the news on the small black-and-white TV they had found in a second-hand store on Grand Avenue. The presenter was young and Reine had never seen his face, but she never watched TV. She didn't even have one in her new studio. He could have become the new anchorman six months ago, for all she knew.

Reine walked to the couch, closely followed by Nola, and sat next to Papa. They all remained quiet for a moment, the only sound filling the room coming from the TV.

At last, Papa asked, still watching the TV, "What's on your mind, Reine?"

She sighed. "I think I don't want to work at C3 anymore."

"Oh," Nola said. "But you just joined the company. Is it because of the murder?"

Reine winced as she heard the word *murder*. "That's the thing. I don't think *anybody* murdered Isaline. I've got reasons to believe Max Caldwell knows it's a safety accident, and he's been tampering with evidence and bribing cops so the word doesn't get out."

"That's something serious, what you're saying," Papa said. "What makes you believe that?"

Reine explained her recent discoveries about the CCTV recordings and her troubling conversations with Elante, Caldwell, and Novau. "I know it's probably not enough to convince another police officer. Maybe a journalist...."

"You need something irrefutable, sweetheart. If what you say is true, you want to be taken seriously."

As Papa stated the obvious, a picture of the C3 tower appeared on the upper left part of the screen with the words "suspect arrested" underneath, and the anchorman said, "The police said they have made significant progress in investigating the sudden death of Isaline Caldwell, enmagineer and niece of C3 CEO Max Caldwell. A suspect has been arrested this evening in what is now being officially investigated as a homicide."

A video of the suspect being escorted by officers into the police station played as the anchorman continued to explain the suspect was a former C3 employee.

"That's Minati," Reine said, shaking her head as she recognized the woman's face despite her attempts to look away from the pressing cameras.

The anchorman then said, "Chief of Police Esias Vilmer gave a press conference earlier tonight, in which he shared his investigating team's findings," as a man in a police uniform behind a podium appeared on screen. Several police officers stood behind him, among them Novau, whose face betrayed a blend of excitement and nervousness.

"Today we have arrested Lou Minati," the police chief said, "for the murder of Isaline Caldwell. Ms. Caldwell's autopsy revealed that the cause of death was copsiamine poisoning, and our investigation revealed that Ms. Minati, who worked at C3 and showed signs of violence toward the victim in the past, possessed large amounts of the drug in her apartment. It is believed the suspect poisoned the victim over the course of several meals shared on the company premises, and exposed Ms. Caldwell to a lethal dose in the hours preceding her death."

"Bullshit!" Reine exclaimed as the police chief kept sharing more details about the investigation. She turned to Papa and explained, "Max Caldwell fired her today, saying she was speaking to the press and leaking trade secrets when all she was doing was sharing safety concerns that were ignored by C3. And now she's arrested."

"You sure this woman didn't hurt Ms. Caldwell?" Papa asked.

"She's *severely allergic* to copsiamine," she said, taking the folder with Minati's medical information from her jacket and showing it to Papa.

Papa squinted to read the document. "Where did you get this?"

"In her office. I took it because I suspected they'd do just this: frame her for a murder she didn't commit. All that because they won't let the city know their technology isn't safe."

Papa thought for a moment, then he asked, "Those

test reports, have you seen them?" Reine shook her head, and Papa continued, "If the police won't look into Isaline's computer, then you need to find them yourself. The originals, untampered. Without that, all you have are deductions, and if I trust what your reasoning tells you, serious journalists won't."

Papa was right, and Reine knew it. Even with the CCTV recordings and the recorded call with Novau, she didn't have enough. Her testimony had some value, and the proof of Minati's allergy may be enough to exonerate her, but it wouldn't be enough to prove that Caldwell and Elante had conspired to hide the truth and that Novau was complicit. It wouldn't bring justice to Isaline. Caldwell would simply find another scapegoat. Reine was no luma expert, no detective, no nothing. Just a recently hired head of security who made bizarre discoveries, had troubling conversations, and had perhaps, after all, a wild imagination.

"The only untampered reports would be on Isaline's computer, and it's at the police station," Reine said, sighing. "I'm not going to break into their evidence room to retrieve and analyze it. And that's if they've not already falsified or deleted the reports."

"Didn't she have another device?" Nola asked.

"What do you mean?"

"Nola's right," Papa said. "Didn't she have another computer where she'd receive a copy, maybe? Or one of these new devices—a personal...."

"A personal digital assistant," Nola exclaimed. "You can receive your electronic messages and files on it."

"That's why they're so pricey," Papa snorted. "Fancy gadgets, these things. Perhaps she had something like that and it's still in her home."

"Hold on," Reine said. "Are you suggesting I break into her apartment and search for some maybe-existing device that may have a copy of the reports?"

Papa shrugged. "Sounds easier than breaking into the police station."

"You realize the police searched her place already."

"Maybe they didn't find everything," Nola said.

"Even if they did find a device," Papa said, "maybe they didn't take it for examination and it's still in her apartment. You should take a look."

Nola nodded excitedly. "It's worth a try. And who knows what else you could find?"

"I could get arrested if I get caught."

Papa looked Reine in the eye and said, a knowing smile on his face, "Then don't get caught."

Before her life ended in C3's Core Room, Isaline lived in the Inner Sunrise, a couple of blocks away from her uncle's company.

Her apartment was on the fourteenth floor of the Sundial Tower, the tallest building in the city after the C3 Tower. Reine had actually visited a studio in the Sundial Tower, but didn't apply as the rent was too high. Of course, she didn't know then that she would have lived in the same building as Isaline, and now she wished she'd chosen to apply, as it would have made her upcoming break-in easier.

It hadn't been difficult to find Isaline's address and confirmation that she'd lived alone. Every bit of privacy Isaline used to have died with her, and Reine found the information in the press, along with pictures of the cordoned-off apartment door and its number—1405.

Getting there unnoticed wouldn't be hard either; there were CCTV cameras in the lobby and elevator, but none in the stairwell and on the upper floors. If Reine kept a low profile as she entered the building and walked to the stairs, she could reach Isaline's apartment without drawing unwanted attention.

The challenging part would be entering the apartment without being seen by nosy neighbors. Fortunately, the people living on the uppermost floors were affluent people keeping to themselves, but picking the lock was still risky. If someone came out of their apartment and asked questions, Reine could always say that she worked at C3 and that Max Caldwell sent her to retrieve valuable work-related documents, with the police's authorization, and that she had forgotten the key back in the office. Since some of it was true, and she could prove it with her company badge, it would be convincing enough. At least, she hoped.

She decided to go in the middle of the day, during her lunch break, when most neighbors would be absent from their apartment for work or busy cooking and eating. Her made-up story would be more credible, too, though she hoped she wouldn't run into anybody. Her backpack ready with everything she needed—the tape recorder, a camera, a cap, a flashlight, gloves, a lock pick set, and two disks and a device Nola gave her—Reine headed out to C3.

Either Elante hadn't reported their interaction from the past day to Max Caldwell, or Caldwell was too busy to summon Reine into his office to tell her how disappointed he was. Good, Reine thought, because she wasn't in the mood to put on an act and apologize, and it was too soon to share her own disappointment and quit. If she truly wanted to make a difference in solving Isaline's death, she had to keep her job.

The morning went by, uneventful. Reine tried to focus on work but found herself unable to do so, her mind racing with thoughts about what she was about to do. She had learned valuable skills during her time in the BCD, mostly from her official training, but also from *unofficial* training by her peers. A significant fraction of the recruits who served in the BCD beyond the mandatory year had a troubled past, and some had a police record filled with non-violent offenses such as theft or trafficking illicit substances. Serving in the BCD was an opportunity to redeem themselves and find a place in the city better than a prison cell, and Reine had learned useful skills from these young men and women. Except, she had never put these skills into practice to break into someone's apartment.

Don't get caught. It was even more important than keeping her job. What if the police arrested her and accused her of conspiring with Minati? She would make an ideal scapegoat, too, especially after her altercations with Elante and Novau. No, she couldn't let that happen.

When lunchtime arrived, she mentally repeated the steps of her plan, exhaled, and left for the Sundial Tower.

The sun was at its zenith in a cloudless sky when Reine stepped outside of the C3 Tower, and soon she put her cap on, imitating the crowd of citizens overwhelmed by the unusual heat. The sky was so clear that Reine could barely see the crystal's light as she looked toward the top of the tower. *We need that crystal to power the city,* she thought while walking to Isaline's apartment. *But not at any cost.*

She quickly reached the Sundial Tower. It was a twenty-two-story building with balconies that became larger the higher they were located. The studio Reine had visited was on the third floor and also had a balcony, except it would have only fit a long chair, as it was ridiculously small compared to the ones Isaline and her higher-up neighbors had. Still, she wondered how things would have turned out should she have lived there. Would have she met Isaline before her first day at C3? Would have they become friends before becoming colleagues? Could have she prevented her from dying? A stupid thought, Reine knew. There was nothing she could have done to prevent what happened. If she had joined C3 sooner, maybe…even so, her job was security, not safety. The crystal wasn't supposed to be a threat. There were no security measures she could have put in place to protect Isaline from it. But knowing that didn't prevent Reine's mind from going through all these *what if* scenarios, and for a moment she wished she had never met Isaline, her beautiful smile and her haunting blue eyes. A selfish thought, of course. A wish not to have been involved in any of what happened, a wish not to care about Isaline and her fate. Yet there she was, standing in front of the Sundial Tower, ready to break into Isaline's apartment to look for untampered reports she wasn't sure existed, or for whatever secret lay inside the apartment of a dead woman she barely knew but cared about so deeply that it was almost frightening.

Bright City, Shattered

Pushing the invading thoughts away, Reine walked inside the building. It looked as she remembered it: a large lobby with a marble fountain at its center that filled the room with a soothing melody, and big, rounded ceiling lights emitting a pale blue light akin to the crystal's that gave the place an eerie atmosphere.

She didn't linger in the lobby and walked quickly yet casually to the staircase, looking down so the cameras wouldn't record her face hidden under the cap.

The staircase was unexpectedly clean, unlike the one in her own apartment building. For an instant, Reine worried about running into a cleaner as she made her way up, but she didn't and reached the fourteenth floor without trouble. She was breathing rapidly, tired from the stair climbing, and she wished she would have worked out more to stay in shape since she had left the BCD.

Taking a moment to slow her racing heart and thoughts, Reine inhaled and exhaled slowly, carefully. Then she took gloves out of her backpack, put them on, and reached for the door handle, ready to leave the quietness and safety of the staircase for the fourteenth floor and her goal—door 1405.

Sweat dripped down her face as she pushed the door open. Was it because of the stress, or because she had just climbed to the fourteenth floor after walking under the blazing sun? She wasn't sure and suspected stress was the main culprit. She didn't like it, but stress was a normal reaction, she knew. What mattered was her ability to remain focused and controlled, and focused and controlled she was. She might not be in great shape, but she hadn't forgotten her training.

The fourteenth floor was both similar and different from the third floor. Like the floor she could have lived on, it featured a long, straight white-walled corridor with a never-ending row of black doors adorned with golden numbers. The difference was the number of doors and the distance between each of them. On the third floor, doors were close to each other; the doors on the fourteenth floor were well distanced, showing how larger and fewer the apartments were compared to the lower floors.

The smell of rice, fish sauce, garlic, and lime came from one door she passed by, reminding Reine of Mama's cuisine. Mama would make rice for special occasions only, as it was a delicacy imported from distant cities who had the land to cultivate it. Reine doubted the people in the apartment were celebrating anything. They probably just had the means to eat rice every day. As she kept walking in the hallway toward Isaline's apartment, she promised herself that if she succeeded, she would buy the finest rice on the market and some fresh produce for Mama to cook a delicious meal for the entire family.

At last, she reached door 1405. There was no yellow

tape anymore, nor anything else that would make it stand out. It wasn't a crime scene, after all, and the police had already searched the place.

Reine didn't stop and kept walking, listening for any sound that would come from inside the apartment. All was quiet. All she could hear was the sound of a television coming from apartment 1406. The neighbor was watching an action movie according to loud bangs coming from inside. Good. Hopefully, they would be too busy following the action to mind what was happening in the hallway.

Reine went back to the door and grabbed a couple of lock picks from her jacket's inner pocket. Before using them, she knocked on the door. Isaline had lived alone, but another Caldwell could be inside, cleaning up the apartment. Better to ensure she wouldn't find herself face to face with a family member who'd call the police on her for breaking and entering. After nobody came to open the door, she tried the doorknob, just in case. Locked, as expected. Quickly, she started picking the lock, her eyes scanning the hallway for anybody coming her way.

A dog barked, startling her. The barking came from a neighbor's apartment—the one where someone was watching a movie. Reine paused. The dog kept barking and a male voice said, "Stop it, Grita!" but the dog didn't listen and kept barking behind the door.

Reine inhaled and started picking the lock again, silently cursing the dog, who must have smelled her. She was almost done when she heard the male voice again, this time right behind the door.

"Is that you, Berto?"

The dog was growling now, barking only every few seconds. Reine needed to decide now: leave and try again another time, or pick that damn lock and get inside Isaline's apartment in the next few seconds. Her mind told her to stop and leave, but she didn't and kept working on the lock. She could do it. It was a simple lock. She was almost there.

Her heart skipped a beat when she heard the neighbor unlock his own door. That's also when she managed to turn the doorknob, and opened the door of Isaline's apartment, rushing inside and closing the door behind her as quietly as she could, while she heard the neighbor walk outside of his apartment and call again for Berto. She feared the dog would come to Isaline's door and bark, but the neighbor scolded his dog, telling her to keep quiet and that Berto—whoever that was—wasn't there, before going back into his apartment, the dog still growling.

Despite having her eye on the peephole, Reine didn't see any of it but heard it all, and let out a long, slow sigh after it was over. She had made it without being caught. Not yet, at least. She wasn't finished.

She turned to the wall and checked for an alarm system. There wasn't one. It was a relief, because she didn't think she could have used the device Nola gave her. It could have disarmed most simple alarm systems, Nola had explained, but Reine preferred that there was no alarm at all, as she didn't feel confident in her ability to follow Nola's instructions properly. Nola was the expert, and she wasn't there. She had offered to join, but Reine said no, of course. Dragging one more person into this mess, and her own sister? It was out of the question.

Reine took out her flashlight. The entrance hall was dimly lit by sunlight coming from the living room, but Reine didn't want to turn on the lights or open more curtains.

She walked toward the living room, her flashlight revealing pictures on the walls. One showed Isaline wearing a lab coat over gray jeans and a blouse, standing next to other C3 employees. Reine recognized Elante among the people in the picture, but the others weren't familiar to her. Isaline looked younger in it—in her early twenties, Reine guessed—so it was likely only she and Elante had remained employed by C3, the others having left the company since the picture was taken. Isaline's youthful face made the age difference between them more obvious, making Reine wonder if Elante had ever been resentful of having a younger manager.

Another picture showed a young Isaline and her grandmother, Florence Caldwell, holding each other affectionately, reminding Reine of how C3 was truly a family business. Isaline would have surely become C3's next CEO had she lived long enough to see her uncle retire. That thought made Reine wonder if Max Caldwell had reasons not to want Isaline to be his successor, if some family quarrel had happened behind closed doors, and if this was why he hadn't seemed affected by his niece's death. Reine couldn't picture him voluntarily causing it, but she could very well imagine him unmoved, and perhaps, *not unhappy* about her passing. After all, he seemed more annoyed by the investigation than afflicted by her death.

The living room was four or five times larger than Reine's studio, with two faux chandeliers hanging from exposed beams. They were off, but natural light filtered through sheer curtains, illuminating the room enough for Reine to turn off the flashlight. She clipped it to her belt and focused on the room. It was untidy, but not as if the police had violently ransacked the place. Whatever they had searched for, they left the place in a relatively normal state; Isaline had probably just been too busy to sort and put away the magazines spread over the coffee table. Piles of books covered the floor next to the couch, on which several coats were spread out. The dining table, right behind the couch, was even more untidy than the coffee table: open boxes of cereal lay around next to piles of plates and glasses, half of them dirty. There was even a bowl half-filled with cereal, a spoon resting carelessly on it. Fortunately, no milk filled the bowl, preventing the apartment from being filled with stench.

Reine felt uneasy. She was inside Isaline's apartment, prying on her personal life, and the dead woman couldn't even object to it. The dead couldn't take offense, Reine knew, but it didn't prevent her from feeling ashamed of her curiosity. What made her even more uneasy was how Isaline's apartment hadn't been cleaned up after her death. Since the police already searched the place, why did her family take so long to clean it up? Certainly, it would take them a long time to pack all her belongings and dispose of it, but the cereal bowl made Reine think that *nobody* had cleaned up at all. Whoever in the Caldwell family was going to take care of the apartment, they hadn't even started. This saddening observation made Reine realize that of all the pictures she had seen on the walls, none of them showed Isaline with Max Caldwell or with other prominent family members. The only picture with another Caldwell was the one with her grandmother, who had now been dead for ten years. There was also no picture of Isaline with friends or with a significant other. Had she been leading a lonely life? Was it why nobody cared to clean a single bowl? Had she been, like Galano said, *a bully*, and hadn't made any friends because of that? Even if Isaline had been someone difficult to work with—which Reine had a hard time fathoming—that wouldn't explain why she wouldn't have made at least a few friends, or been close to other Caldwells. Isaline had not only died alone; she had lived alone, too, and now her memory was falling into oblivion.

Reine remembered that she hadn't come to mourn Isaline, and that she had a mission: finding a device that could contain an unaltered copy of the reports.

She searched the living room carefully, hoping to find a portable computer hidden under each magazine or book she lifted, but there was nothing. She looked into the coats for a personal digital assistant inside a pocket, but she only found used subway tickets and packs of tissues. The wooden cabinet on which a large TV stood gave no better results. Reine even looked behind the three paintings hanging on the walls for a hidden safe, but all she could see was the beige wallpaper. Not wanting to give up the search of the living room so quickly, she pulled a chair and climbed on it, so she could have a good view on the top side of the beams, but a disappointing emptiness covered in dust welcomed her.

Clicking her tongue, she went down and scanned the room for anything she'd missed. There, under the coffee table and the couch! A carpet. She lifted it and tried the floorboards for some secret cache. Again, nothing. Just the plain and boring floor.

She exhaled. What if she had taken all these risks for nothing? It was a possibility, of course, but finding nothing meant giving up on the truth. It meant giving up on Isaline. Papa was right; without substantial proof, her claims were as good as slander. No, she had to keep looking. She had only searched the living room. Perhaps she would find something in the kitchen or in the bedroom.

The kitchen was the closest room, so that's where she pursued her search. She found it surprisingly clean, but when she opened the fridge, she understood why: there was barely any food inside it. Just some milk and food leftovers in airtight plastic boxes. The trash can contained plastic bags and cardboard takeout boxes labeled with the names of local restaurants and food trucks. Isaline must have barely used the kitchen to cook. Reine searched every cupboard and drawer for a device, but her search was, again, unfruitful.

On her way to the bedroom, she searched a closet, but there was nothing besides a few old brooms, a vacuum cleaner, a bucket and a mop. Reine continued to the bedroom, but stopped a moment before pushing the door open. Searching the living room and the kitchen was one thing; Isaline's bedroom was another, and an uncomfortable one. The most private aspects of her life were behind that door, and again, Reine felt uneasy at the tingling of curiosity it aroused in her. She had never planned on breaking into Isaline's apartment—or anyone's—until the previous day, and now she knew why she would never do it again: it made her feel *dirty*.

But she had a good reason to do it, and it was all for Isaline, so she pushed the unpleasant feeling aside and opened the door. Seeing that the shutters were closed and the room pitch black, she turned on her flashlight. Inside, she found what everybody would expect in a bedroom: a bed, a nightstand, and a chest of drawers. There was a pillbox on the nightstand, for what Reine supposed was copsiamine. Examining it, she noticed each compartment contained two tablets. Reine didn't know if it represented a lot of copsiamine or not. She opened the two drawers, finding pajamas carefully folded in the bottom drawer, and several bottles of copsiamine in the top one. She counted six of them, each containing a hundred and fifty tablets, which seemed to be a lot, even if taking two tablets a day. Why did Isaline stock so many bottles in advance? Reine grabbed a bottle and looked at the expiration date. It expired in nine months. She checked the others; they all expired at the same date. At two pills per day, half of the tablets in the bottles would be expired by then. Reine gulped. Could Isaline have purposefully…*no*, she stopped herself. *I don't know anything about Pabst's disease and copsiamine.*

Perhaps Isaline needed to adjust the treatment and took more tablets sometimes. Yes, this was probably it. Reine still took out her camera to take a picture. Then she closed the drawer and left the copsiamine bottles alone, resuming her search for a device.

There was nothing under the bed. She tried the chest of drawers, feeling once again uneasy as she looked through Isaline's clothing. Unlike the books, magazines, coats, and cereal boxes that were lying around in the living room, Isaline's blouses, t-shirts, skirts, and jeans were carefully folded and organized. Reine tried not to disorganize the clothes, as she didn't want anybody to know someone had searched the place, but also because it seemed disrespectful to Isaline. It was silly, but she still made sure every piece of clothing was back in its place when she closed the drawers.

She had found nothing. She sat on the bed, the flash-light pointed toward the wall, forming a large circle of light against the pale flowery wallpaper. There was no device. No saved copy of untampered reports. She had come for nothing. Minati would go to jail for Isaline's murder and Reine would never know the truth. And, she thought, it may all have been her wild imagination, after all.

She had one last room to check before leaving—only to be sure she had really come for nothing and had no regrets leaving Isaline's apartment empty handed. Isaline's bedroom had its own attached bathroom, and it was the most luxurious room of the apartment. It had both a shower and a bathtub, and a marble washstand that looked like it came straight out of a home decor magazine.

Reine checked the bathroom cabinet, only finding

towels and reserves of soap and shampoo. What did she expect, really? To find a hidden personal digital assistant wrapped in a towel? Exhaling, she glanced at the metallic magazine holder next to the toilet bowl. It contained books and magazines of all sorts, but there wasn't any device squeezed in between.

A large, thick book intrigued Reine. She grabbed it and sat on the bathroom floor, looking at the cover. Its title read *Principles of Luma-Based Energy: An Introduction to Enmagineering* and written by no one else than Florence Caldwell. It seemed odd that such a beautiful book written by Isaline's grandmother, to whom she had been close, was in the bathroom instead of a bookcase. Reine opened it. On the first page was a dedication to Isaline, signed by Florence Caldwell, that read, "Trust the luma, and it will trust you." Reine didn't know how luma could trust someone, so she supposed it was only an enigmatic allegory.

She flipped through the book, not even trying to make sense of its content, which was beyond her understanding, and was about to close it and put it back in the magazine holder when a thin notebook appeared in between two pages. The cover was black and glossy, reflecting the light from the flashlight eerily. Reine opened it and found mathematical formulae and schemata on the first pages. Some notes Isaline had taken while reading the book, Reine thought. She kept flipping through the pages that were filled with more and more notes.

Halfway through the notebook, she stopped on a page that contained notes about dosages for something called "CoAM" which Reine understood was copsiamine. Her stomach clenched as she read Isaline's notes. Isaline had documented her treatment and the number of tablets she was taking every day in the month preceding her death, and it was *not* two tablets a day. It was more. Way more, some days. Four weeks before her death, she had documented taking four tablets before running a safety test, writing, "Unsuccessful. Will try a more powerful surge and increase CoAM to five tablets in two days." Two more dates that same week had similar notes, with up to six copsiamine tablets documented.

Reine dropped the notebook and ran her fingers through her hair. Nobody had poisoned Isaline with copsiamine. Both Max Caldwell and Reine had been so blinded with their respective explanation of Isaline's death that they had ruled out suicide. Reine gulped as the word crossed her mind, but the notes left little doubt about what had happened. Isaline had poisoned herself and used the safety tests to get a fatal power surge to overcome her nervous system and cause a heart attack. But, how? Hadn't Lancy said the tests were run from the console in the small control room? Isaline must have initiated them and walked next to the crystal, Reine guessed. But why? Was it because she was so lonely, despite what Caldwell had said about Isaline having everything she wished for? And why commit suicide at work, using the crystal? And why document it?

Reine exhaled. Something didn't add up. Why would Isaline need to take high doses of copsiamine? Wouldn't the power surge be enough to kill anybody too close, with or without taking extra copsiamine? Or the other way around—take a massive dose of copsiamine and wait for her heart to stop all by itself, outside of the Core Room? And why increase the dose progressively and not take an entire bottle at once? She went back to reading the notes, turning the pages so she could see what happened day by day until Isaline's death. Isaline had kept doing the same thing—taking high doses of copsiamine before running a test—until the very end, and her notes became increasingly cryptic.

It was when Reine reached the notes Isaline took the day before her death that everything finally became clear. Isaline didn't take the copsiamine to poison herself. She took it to *protect* herself from the crystal. Reine couldn't believe what she was reading, but she knew it was about to change everything, not only at C3, but in the entire city.

Isaline had tried to protect herself from the crystal because it was *upset*. And she had told Max Caldwell, who had asked her to *kill* it.

Bright City, Shattered

Allie hadn't yet started her day when Reine walked into C3's lobby. Nobody sat at her desk to welcome visitors—who couldn't have entered anyway, since the doors opened only to employees' badges before seven in the morning. It was excellent, because Reine wasn't in the mood for morning small talk with anybody.

The building wasn't empty. Some scientists were already working in the labs, and security contractors covered the night shift until Orlan and Maia arrived. What mattered was that Caldwell and Elante weren't there and wouldn't interfere with her plans. Once she was done, Reine couldn't care less about running into them, but now wasn't the time.

The elevator took her to the thirtieth floor in twenty-two seconds that felt like twenty-two hours. As the stainless-steel doors opened, she reached for the bottle of copsiamine in her pocket, but didn't take it out. She couldn't be recorded on camera handling copsiamine, much less a bottle labeled for Isaline. She walked to the women's bathroom and locked herself in the largest stall. There, she opened the copsiamine bottle and put a tablet in her hand.

She didn't swallow it. Instead, she looked at the tablet, hesitating. She had learned from Isaline's notes that if copsiamine was dangerous when consumed in high doses, it was because it tried *too much* to counteract the effect of luma on one's body, causing a needless overstimulation of the nervous system. But if there *was* a sudden, intense luma shock, copsiamine was the only thing that could save someone from an almost certain death. Isaline and other enmagineers had fed the crystal with luma slowly over four decades, but it was now so full of it that it could inflict luma shocks and hurt people at will.

At will. Reine had a hard time believing it, but it was the problem Isaline had discovered. The crystal was upset because it had gained a will of its own. Isaline had discovered it recently and hadn't known exactly when it started. In her notes, she had estimated six months ago, but it could have been longer, since the crystal hadn't reached consciousness overnight. It had been a slow process that went undetected until it was too late.

First, Isaline had noticed an unusual, inexplicable flickering of the crystal when she was feeding it luma. It happened occasionally in the beginning but had become more frequent as weeks passed. Then, whispers. Unintelligible, barely audible whispers that she thought were benign disturbances in the murmur, but soon she had understood actual *words.* They didn't seem to come from the crystal, and for a time Isaline had questioned her sanity, but she could only hear them in the Core Room. She had tried to answer, to ask questions, but every time the whispers would cease, as if scared by Isaline's voice. The last clue was what Minati had herself noticed, that Isaline had known and tried to downplay per Max Caldwell's orders: inconsistencies in the energy flow from the crystal. The production of electricity would sometimes slow down inexplicably, but as soon as Isaline, Elante, or another enmagineer would walk inside the Core Room, it would go back to normal, although they hadn't done anything yet.

Isaline's suspicions were confirmed when, one day, while feeding luma to the crystal, she received a mild but excruciating luma shock followed by hateful whispered words. It had never happened before. The shock hadn't harmed her beyond pain, but only thanks to her copsi-amine treatment. Another enmagineer could have been hurt or even died.

That day, she had met with Max Caldwell to come up with a plan. What could they do with a giant angry crystal when an entire city depended on its goodwill for energy? Isaline and Caldwell had disagreed. Isaline wanted to release a large amount of luma back into the world, hoping it would lower the sentience of the crystal, but that meant a smaller crystal, and a smaller energy supply for a hungri-er-than-ever city, so it wasn't an option for Caldwell. He, instead, wanted her to kill its consciousness while keeping all the accumulated luma intact, and that's what Isaline had tried to do by running intense safety tests to overpower the crystal while containing its luma all by herself, leaving the safety of the control room to do so and risking her life every single time.

Until it killed her.

Fuck Max Caldwell was all Reine could think as she contemplated the copsiamine in her hand. *Fuck him and his ambitions and his lies.* C3 was rotten to the core because of him, and what was once the revolutionary company of a smart, environment-friendly Florence Caldwell had become a greedy place where results mattered more than everything else. They mattered more than the truth. More than family.

Reine put the tablet in her mouth and swallowed, then left the stall and went to the sink to drink several mouthfuls of water, hoping her body wouldn't overreact. Since she didn't have Pabst's disease, one tablet seemed reasonable; more would certainly be dangerous. But she was no physician, and Elante would perhaps find her dead in the Core Room in a few hours. Or the crystal would attack her, and she would survive thanks to the copsiamine in her body.

Reine put safety glasses on and left the bathroom.

The floor was empty. It didn't have any offices or lab space, as half of it was used for the Core Room, and the other half for the bathroom and the building's ventilation system. Reine entered the Core Room with anxiety and excitement as her sole companions.

Inside, the low humming of the crystal and its blinding light greeted her. She closed the door behind her and walked straight to the control room, trying not to think about how close she was to a giant murderous crystal.

She could access the Core Room and enter its control room, but couldn't use the console itself, even with her security clearance level. Only enmagineers like Isaline or Elante could use it. Even Max Caldwell couldn't use it. The only thing out of his reach. But Reine didn't need to use the console. She was in the control room because it was the only place where she could install her camcorder and hope the image wouldn't be completely white, thanks to the tinted glass pane.

Audio would be an issue, though, but she had bought a compatible wireless microphone which would allow the camcorder to record her conversation with the crystal—if it was willing to talk, of course. Despite the whispering, none of Isaline's notes had mentioned a successful interaction with the crystal, but with a bit of persuasion, perhaps it would answer Reine.

Once her installation was ready, Reine left the control room and walked back to the crystal. Again, the low humming filled her ears, and she squinted as she tried to look at the crystal. It looked so normal, so inert, that for an instant Reine wondered if Isaline had been right. There was only one way to be certain, so she said, "I am in the Core Room of Clean Crystal Corporation, most commonly known as C3." She was saying it for the recording, but also because it sounded foolish to start by *greeting* the crystal.

The crystal kept humming smoothly, its tone and brilliance unperturbed. Would it react in any way? Did it know Reine was there? Could it *hear* and *understand* her?

Reine continued, "I am here to show the crystal is *aware* and dangerous."

Nothing happened.

"I believe it killed Isaline Caldwell."

The crystal flickered, making Reine raise her eyebrows. Had it…understood the accusations, or was it just a coincidence?

"It killed Isaline Caldwell because she was trying to shut the crystal's awareness down. She was trying to hurt it."

It flickered twice, and this time, Reine's instinct told her Isaline had been right. The crystal could understand her. But would it talk to her? A flickering crystal wouldn't be enough to convince the public. Her notebook was a crucial piece of evidence, but Caldwell could easily dismiss it, and Isaline wasn't there anymore to defend her claim. Reine needed something big.

"I also believe she didn't want to hurt it, but she was forced to."

It didn't flicker.

"I'm a friend of Isaline, but I don't want to harm the crystal. I want to understand it." It flickered again and Reine continued, speaking softly, "I'm not an enmagineer. I can't hurt you. I only want to talk."

Please, she wanted to add, but she didn't have time to do so because a crackling voice filled the room and said, "Talk."

Reine froze. *For heavens' sake,* she thought. *Isaline was right.* She had been right, and Reine had managed *to make it talk.* But she couldn't pinpoint the origin of the voice. It sounded like it came from *everywhere.* For an instant she even wondered if the voice spoke inside her head, if the crystal was telepathic—or if she was insane—but it repeated itself with a stronger voice that made Reine's entire body vibrate, confirming it was truly speaking, and that the camcorder must have recorded it.

"TALK."

For a giant crystal that had refused to interact with Isaline, it now sounded impatient to speak.

Reine gulped. "How long have you been aware?"

"Forever," it said, to Reine's surprise.

"Forever? Since Florence created you?"

"Yes."

Reine couldn't believe it. Isaline had written that…. Well, whatever she had written, she must have underestimated the extent of her discovery, and Reine now had the opportunity to fully uncover it, so she asked, "How?"

"Luma is awareness."

Reine frowned. Luma, awareness? What did it mean? Luma was everywhere, flowing in every living thing, flowing in the air. Reine remembered the doomsday preacher from the Newtown District. Could have he been right, somehow?

"Luma is making you aware?"

"No."

The crystal wasn't making things easy, but Reine couldn't expect a giant crystal to go on a lengthy explanation. It seemed that it could only respond with simple yesses and nos and brief sentences. She let out a long sigh, thinking about her next question. If luma wasn't making it aware, but luma was awareness....

"You are actually not the crystal."

"Correct."

"You are the luma itself."

"Yes."

Everything made sense now. The crystal was only a receptacle, a vessel converting luma into power. "Does the crystal hurt you?"

"It kills us. It kills us forever."

An endless torture. Luma was aware of itself, and its particles were trapped inside the crystal for days, weeks, perhaps even months, until they eventually burned. An endless death. Enmagineers had fed so much of it to the crystal that the accumulated luma was strong enough to grow resentful and become dangerous.

Reine gulped and said, "You want it to stop."

"Yes."

"How do we make it stop?"

"Free us."

"You cannot leave the crystal?"

"Not far. It always takes us back. Free us."

That's how it could hurt people in the Core Room, but was unable to flee C3 on its own. Isaline had been right to want to free some luma. Of course she had been. Even if the luma hadn't told her, she had been smart enough to understand what was happening and what the best solution was. If only Caldwell had listened to her.

"I'm not an enmagineer. I will need some help to free you."

"Then find help."

Reine paused. The luma had spoken in a low, almost threatening voice. She had to be very careful with her next words if she didn't want to receive a deadly shock.

"I will find help, I promise. But before I go, I have more questions."

"Ask. Then find help."

"Did you kill Isaline Caldwell?"

"Yes," it answered. "She hurt us."

Reine closed her eyes and inhaled deeply. "Could have she been successful? Could have she killed your consciousness and made you inert?"

"Luma is awareness."

"I guess this means no," Reine whispered. "One last question. Are we conscious because of luma?"

"Luma is awareness."

Reine didn't respond. Instead, she walked back to the control room, stopped her camcorder and removed the cassette from it. On it was the proof not only that Max Caldwell had lied about the crystal being safe, but also that the entire city was doomed.

Caldwell finally heard about Reine's interaction with Elante, because he called Reine on the same day, asking why in the world she wasn't at work anymore and to come immediately to his office for an urgent one-on-one meeting.

"I don't think I'm going to do that."

"Are you resigning, Reine?" His voice was flat, not even disappointed. It was the voice of a man who had had enough and wanted to be done. At least, they had something in common.

"Yeah, I'm done. Goodbye Max."

With that, Reine hung up and called the *Daily Light*.

"Why didn't you find an enmagineer to help?" Nola asked as she walked through sea-gate number four.

Reine sighed, following her sister through the gate, and said, "Freeing the luma meant putting the city in the dark and sending us forty years back. I couldn't make that choice for ten million people." Not to mention that she would have had to find an enmagineer who'd believed her *and* was willing to go against Max Caldwell. "The city has to decide."

"But it's hurting, and it killed Isaline!"

"I know," Reine said, her heart sinking as she thought about Isaline, "and now *everybody* knows. We'll have to make a decision, eventually. All of us." *If only we could have made it before Isaline died,* Reine thought. *She would still be here with us. With me.*

Nola clicked her tongue. "What if we decide to keep the crystal and never release the luma?"

"Well," Reine said as they reached the beach, "I don't think anybody wants to approach the crystal to feed it luma anymore. Even if the city and C3 decide to keep the crystal, they won't find enough enmagineers to make it work."

Elante had been the first to resign after the *Daily*

Light's bombshell news. He even called Reine to apologize for what he had done, tacitly admitting that Reine had been right about her accusations. He hadn't known about the crystal and luma, Elante had said over the phone. Reine didn't know if this was true. Perhaps Elante had ignored the problem until he learned that it was bigger than Isaline had imagined. It didn't matter, anyway. Max Caldwell resigned from C3 after the city initiated a lawsuit against him, and the police released Minati and fired Novau, so there had been some justice. Reine could live with Elante getting away with what he had done.

"Even if no one cares about the luma hurting, it's too dangerous," Reine said. "Other companies have been trying to find some new techs for a while now, some very promising."

"Do you think one will succeed at replacing the crystal?"

"They have to."

Seagulls flew over Reine and Nola, squealing and laughing and diving into the peaceful ocean. It was hard for Reine to imagine that a few weeks ago, a wave had submerged the beach and wiped away the family house.

"Can you tell me now why you wanted to go to the beach?" Nola asked.

Reine nodded. "I'm tired of people chasing me in the city. The beach is the only place they leave me alone."

Bright City, Shattered

The place was indeed quiet, except for a few volunteers cleaning up the last remaining debris, who were too busy to pay attention to Reine and Nola. Reine's recording from the Core Room wasn't the cause of her recent fame—the image was too bright for her face to be recognizable—but tabloids had quickly found her and published her picture for the entire city to see. Now, half of Bright City revered her as a courageous whistleblower, and the other half hated her for putting their luma-reliant lifestyle at risk. As for the mayor-president, he had tried to convince Reine to talk again to the crystal. A handful of people had been brave enough to enter the Core Room and risk a deadly luma shock to try bargaining with the crystal—or, more accurately, with the luma—but it wouldn't engage in negotiations and would repeat the same request it had asked Reine, over and over. *Free us.*

Reine refused, of course. She had no desire to convince a sentient entity to keep being enslaved. C3's remaining enmagineers had theorized that by freeing half of the luma and allowing the crystal to shrink to a smaller size, there wouldn't be enough luma to be dangerous to enmagineers—confirming what Isaline had known all along. The electricity production would dramatically decrease, but that would be better than freeing all the luma altogether and stopping the production. But that didn't change the fact that *luma was awareness*, and that it was *wrong* to burn it like coal in a furnace. No, Reine wouldn't become complicit in an endless torture. She wouldn't allow a single atom of luma to be harmed because of her, and hundreds of thousands of citizens—including the deputy mayor herself—agreed with her stance. Bright City had to find another way to power itself.

"Why don't you come live with us in the Big District?" Nola asked.

"And bring journalists and stalkers to your door? Forget it."

"I'll shoo them away, you don't worry," Nola said, an impish smile on her face.

Typical Nola, Reine thought, smiling back at her. "I was actually thinking about building a new beach house," she said softly as she stopped walking.

"A new beach house? With what money?"

"With the one I could get from all these TV hosts who are dying to have me on their show."

"I thought you didn't want to go on TV."

Reine shrugged. "If that allows us to get a new house, I can do it."

"No," Nola said. "Don't bother. Plus, I like the Big District. And I think Papa is finally getting used to it."

"Really?"

"Oh, he still complains about the apartment, but you know him. He complains about everything. He complained about the sand and the wind and the water being too cold or too hot when we were still living here." Nola gestured toward the west, where their beach house used to be.

"True," Reine said. "So, we're staying in the city, I guess."

"At least for now. But we can always change our minds and come back. The beach isn't going anywhere."

Nola stretched her arms and untied her bun. The wind immediately blew her hair, pushing it against her face. Then she took off her shoes and walked to the ocean until the water reached her ankles.

"Right," Reine said as she took off her own shoes. "It's not going anywhere."

Acknowledgements

It takes many people to bring a book to readers. I'd like to thank my spouse Félix, who not only supports my writing career like no one else but also said this novella is his favorite story of all the ones I've written. My publisher, Robert Lewis, for believing in Bright City and its unusual genre blending. All my friends for supporting me, in particular my fellow writer friends at Book Inkers and other amazing Bay Area writing groups. And you, for reading this book. You are the reason I keep writing stories. Thank you!

About the Author

Millie Abecassis is a writer of speculative fiction originally from France. She is a graduate of the Panthéon-Sorbonne University and now works in the biotech industry. Her debut novella, Daughters of the Blue Moon, was published in 2025. Bright City, Shattered is her second novella. She is the founder of #SmallPitch and the co-founder of the Small Spec Book Awards. Millie lives in San Jose, California with her husband and their cats. You can learn more about her writing and other endeavors at millieabecassis.com.

Also Available from Polymath Press

Ghost Girls and Rabbits by Cassondra Windwalker

Flush with the victory of winning the election as Alaska's first Athabaskan Senator, Noni Begay wakes to find herself buried alive. When her coffin lid opens, though, it's not to rescue but to six years of captivity, betrayed by the one person she trusted most. Escape will require not only all her strength but all the strength and stories of the ancestors she had until now imagined were only a useful device, an accessory she wore to win votes and social media followers.

Mary Nelson's only daughter, Ryska, went missing ten years ago, with no one but her mother to search for her. Having used up every favor and chit she has, Mary is willing to risk everything on one last ploy to save her daughter from the monsters...even if she has to become one herself.

A chilling psychological horror novel excoriating the epidemic of missing and murdered indigenous women and girls in North America, Ghost Girls and Rabbits is an unforgettable read perfect for fans of Scandinavian noir and literary horror, told by two fractured minds in the trappings of myths truer than mirrors.

Arithmophobia: An Anthology of Mathematical Horror edited by Robert Lewis

"Arithmophobia," *n.*: The fear of numbers or mathematics.

Whether you love mathematics or find it terrifying, this anthology of original tales of terror is sure to send a chill down your spine. With an unlucky thirteen brand new horror stories and a bonus poem in case any readers suffer from triskaidekaphobia, these pages combine the talents of some of the genre's most experienced award-winning practitioners of terror and some of the literary world's most promising new voices.

These stories tell us of strange and horrifying new geometries, crazed and violent mathematicians, sentient and malevolent numbers, and even some new mathematical twists on some classic monsters. You needn't be a mathematician to experience these new forms of mathematical terror, though students of the discipline might recognize some familiar names and ideas lurking in the shadows.

So pull up a chair, dust off your abacus and slide rule, and prepare to experience… *Arithmophobia.*